Mylok:
Overlord of Earth

Mylok:

Overlord of Earth

Thorpe E. Wright V

authorHOUSE®

AuthorHouse™
1663 Liberty Drive
Bloomington, IN 47403
www.authorhouse.com
Phone: 1 (800) 839-8640

Cover and illustrations by Thorpe E. Wright V

Published by AuthorHouse   09/07/2016

ISBN: 978-1-5246-1785-1 (sc)
ISBN: 978-1-5246-1783-7 (hc)
ISBN: 978-1-5246-1784-4 (e)

Library of Congress Control Number: 2016911148

Print information available on the last page.

This book is printed on acid-free paper.

To my sister, *Leslie,* without her help,
this book would have never been done.
To my parents, for their encouragement
and support.

Prologue

The scorching sun, high in the noon sky, pounds on the back of thousands of men and mere boys. They are enslaved crop workers tilling in dust fields along the Nile River. Most of them have scars upon their backs from the lash of Pre-Egyptian slave masters. A father and son working side by side tear at the dry dirt with stones and their callused hands. They continue to dig for what seems to be an eternity. Finally, a small hole is created. A tiny seed is placed inside, then covered. It is hoped it will grow much needed food. Rain has not been seen for months. There is often nothing to help the starving.

One man faints from the exhausting heat. He is sworn at by a soldier and lashed to the point of death. As if nothing is happening, the two slaves continue with their work. There is no mercy for those who stop. Hundreds of slaves die every week. The father looks to his son, who is hard at work, while kneeling in the dry dirt and pebbles. The young man is just beginning to show the first signs of a good beard. All slaves have beards and long hair. A shaven face is the sign of a Master of the Lash. Masters have white robes with colored sashes around their waist. They all have wooden sandals to protect their feet from the burning ground. Very few slaves have any clothing besides a piece of cloth to cover their genitals. Anything considered a luxury is stolen by the Masters.

The father slave glares at the yellow ball of fire high in the sky and quickly stretches out his hand to block the irritating rays of the sun. He explores the heavens for a single cloud. Yet, he finds none. Only an empty ocean of blue sky. He shakes his head in disgust. The man squeezes his black beard in hopes of recovering a drop of sweat--anything to quench his great thirst for water. He has not had a drop for two days. Every now and then he eats a seed when the guards are not watching. However, his guilt and his logic prevent him from eating all of them. With luck, these seeds will someday feed all.

The skeleton-of-a-man knows his days are numbered. Again, he looks to the heavens in the search of hope. In a daze, he utters to himself, "God, for the sake of my only remaining son, give us rain so that he can live."

The lash finds him quickly. "Back to work!" the Lash Master yells.

The young man rushes to save his father's hide. The teenager begs for forgiveness and asks the Master for water. "Please forgive my father! He needs water!" the young slave says to the Master. The shaven face laughs. All Masters know that water cannot be given to a sick man. The Master turns his back and walks away. The slave stands up and looks all around for a water carrier as he stands by his dying father. There are none to be found. The son of the doomed kneels down and lifts his father's head from the hot ground. The cursed slave begins to cry; he knows the end is near for his father.

While laying on the burning ground, the bearded man looks upward at the sad face and smiles as a sign of hope. In last words to his son, he says, "Malik...Have heart on these men...Don't be like your brothers! Leave this place so that you can have a family...Become a powerful man." Tears overwhelm the son as his father falls into eternal sleep. As the last of his family and tribe, Malik is now truly alone!

Night soon sweeps the sky. The moon is full, and many of the slaves are asleep in the fields. A few are restless--as is Malik. He stares at the moon for many hours, remembering what his father had told him. A smile crosses Malik's face as he thinks he sees his father's face in the moon. It is time to leave this place of hell. Malik thinks, If I stay here, I will surely die like the others. He sits up. His eyes scan the fields for any guards. There are none in sight. There's no need for any. Where could he go? He thinks, I can't go to the city for they will kill me for running away. That also includes going toward the ocean. Also, the ocean is too heavily guarded. His only choice is through the desert. However, only a fool would do such a thing. How could he survive? The lack of water and the hot sun would kill him. However, if he stayed, the same was also true. The desert, at least, gave him a chance for survival.

The young man, while in his late teens, soon finds himself walking the lonely journey through the desert, following his father's moonlit smile. All through the night he continues to walk.

Hours later, the burning sun begins to creep upon the young man's back. All hope begins to wither as his father's figure disappears with the cooling night. The sun grows hotter than Malik ever imagined it could. The sun is soon over his head. Which way to go? The sky seems to spin. The ground appears to become a vapor of steam. The hot desert sand grows unbearable to his blistering feet. Then, the ground seems to jump. He has fallen to his knees. Unable to continue, he figures it is time for eternal sleep. Soon, he thinks, he will be with his beloved family within the stars.

A sound of thunder awakens the young man at night from another dimension to what appeared to be reality. The cooling night aids comfort to his tired body. The teen jumps to his feet with joy and throws his hands into the air in the shape of a "Y." Could it be? Rain? No, he thinks to himself. Lightning never had such brilliant colors or shapes. He looks overhead and sees only stars in the night sky. Not one cloud blocks his view. His father again smiles from the heavens. In the far distance, the believed storm approaches closer still. Terror overcomes him quickly as the bizarre storm obstructs the moonlit sky. He thinks that lightning has struck him, and he tries to scream for mercy to the gods. Yet, no sound is heard!

Immediately, he finds himself in a room with several other beings, except they look like Masters. They all have shaven faces. Stranger still, they have no hair on their heads. The foreheads were too large for their faces. The bodies were covered in a one piece black silken material. Though he is trapped in a continuous lightning storm within a transparent cell, they seem to speak to him through their thoughts. What kind of men are these who have practically no mouths and no protruding private parts? He wonders. What is this place? Surely, this is death and I have gone to the heavens. There is no pain! My hunger, thirst, and feet no longer give me pain...Only my family know me. Who is that calling me by name?

Three of the believed family members take him to another table. There, they open his chest and head. The young patient watches with horror as he looks into the enormous lifeless black eyes of the medicine man. I've been cut open, but there is no pain. In addition, I'm too weak to defend myself, he thinks. His eyes wander around the strange room. Never in his life has he seen walls that shine. So many lights and objects are unknown to him.

While trapped upon the table, an alleged bald brother reaches for a spherical object. There are six fingers on his hand! Without touching the sphere, the sounds become deafening; like a swarm of giant locust. Fire and lightning again hit his chest. The trapped slave is still unable to cry out. Hours seem to pass with no end. Will I look like these hideous creatures when they are through with me? He wonders. Then, he is turned over by an unknown source of energy. For the first time, he realizes that he had never been on the table at all. Colored beams of light shoot from the ceiling and brand a golden cross into his back. Then, a serpent beast is formed, wrapping around the golden cross.

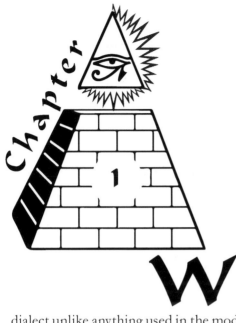

Within a darkly lit room, a young man watches a pretty woman upon a giant screen. In a foreign dialect unlike anything used in the modern world, a voice is heard behind the man. "The male line of the name, Kantorovich, for two generations is gone," a priest said over the shoulder of the man. "She is not the key," the head priest said for the many. "Our fate has already been written."

"Destiny can always be rewritten," the man explained. "My options are few."

"In doing this, you risk all," the priest replied with his head bowed. "May our souls go with you."

"My heart goes with you," twelve more priests said in unison.

Three days later, a young couple sat at a candlelit table in a high class restaurant. In addition, they appeared to be the youngest ones there. All the men were well dressed, wearing two or three piece suits. Some even wore tuxedos. The women wore beautiful gowns. The young man was wearing a black, perfectly fitting three-piece suit. His date, also trying to make a good first impression, showed off her newest dress. It was a gorgeous light green dress with a low cut front.

The young woman couldn't help think her friendly date was too good to be true. Not only is he obviously loaded, she thought to herself, but he's so sure of himself. It was as if he had been dating for a hundred years, as if he knew everything about her. When he looks at me, it's as if he looks through and into me, she thought. Not just at me. It's as if, he's interested in what I am; not just for my looks like other men. There's a good feeling I get from him that I've never felt before. They both continue with their conversation over a romantic sip of wine.

"Mylok," she said with a puzzled look upon her face.

"Yes, Barbara?" he replied with an alluring smile.

"What kind of name is Mylok? Is it Russian or something?"

"No, it's not Russian," he said reassuringly. He hesitated for a moment, thinking of a good choice of words. "It's actually an old Egyptian name."

"Oh, how interesting!" she said with excitement. "Were you born in Egypt?"

"Yes, but I lived there for a very short time."

"Where do you live now?" she asked, trying to find out more about this fascinating man.

"I'm from the Bermuda area."

"I was there!" she exclaimed with joy, grateful to stumble upon a topic they had in common. "It's a beautiful island." Barbara did not want to tell him about her two week trip there, because she wanted to get information out of him. "What part of the island are you from?"

Mylok hesitated in his reply, as if he had something to hide. She looked at him in wonder. Could he have lied to me about living in Bermuda? She thought. Barbara's thoughts quickly changed as he smiled at her, assuring her that he hadn't. He knew the island quite well. He had another sip of wine and then sat back in his chair. In answer to her question, he replied, "I'm not from the Bermuda Island itself, but not too far outside it."

Barbara nodded at his elusive answer. Well, she thought, I don't know him very well, and if he keeps this up, I'll never know him any better. He had come into the restaurant where she worked early that morning. He was all alone. Luckily, things were slow when she waited on him, so there was time to get acquainted. He had a large glass of orange juice, two eggs, and toast, she recalled. It seemed that he was very much alive that morning, unlike all the other customers she usually served during the days she worked. He had a certain charisma.

Mylok even called her by name as if he knew her well. Probably read my name tag she thought. He asked her about the courses she is taking at the university. His dialogs of her courses, and life in general, showed great knowledge. His humorous stories of living life had great depth. Barbara was in awe of his knowledgeable mind.

After talking for about twenty minutes, he had asked her out on a date. Barbara still did not know why she had accepted his offer. However, it was understood that it would be an innocent date of casual conversation. Barbara had already explained to Mylok that morning, she was going steady with another man. Nevertheless, there was something about him. His face and voice were vaguely familiar. Somewhere, in the past, Barbara knew she had met him. Perhaps, it was at some party at the university. Nevertheless, there was a feeling inside telling her that she was indebted to him for something. However, she did not know for what.

While tearing into her lobster, she shook her head, trying to remember exactly how he had asked her for a date. She could not remember. She thought to herself, He was too clever to turn down his invitation. Then the man of her dreams coughed once. She looked up at him. "Are you all right?"

"Fine," he stated, as he drank some ice cold water. To cover up his little embarrassment, he exclaimed, "The shells are a little tricky to watch at times." While staring into her eyes, he added some more romance to the picture by saying, "Looking at you makes me feel much better."

Barbara blushed the color of the lobster claw she held in her hand, and her embarrassment led her to drop the claw in her lap. Not very original, she thought, but it was pleasant of him to say so anyway.

Barbara was deeply touched by his words. "Thank you," Barbara said. At the same time, she casually brushed the lobster claw onto the floor, hoping he did not notice it fall. She then dug into the belly, a little upset at the meat she lost on the floor. Suddenly, she noticed another lobster claw resting on the table on a second bread plate. In wonder, she felt the ground with her foot. She swept the fallen claw with her foot and then stepped on it for reassurance that it had fallen. Yes, it had fallen, she thought.

Barbara looked at the new claw in bewilderment. Then, she looked at Mylok to see him looking at her, this time with half a grin on his face. He winked at her, and she noticed his bread plate was missing. At first, she was embarrassed by her clumsiness. After thinking of his noble gesture, she started to giggle to herself and then broke into a little laughter. He joined in with her laughter. They smiled at each other. Pleased with the new lobster claw, she said, "Thanks a lot...would you like half of it?"

"No, thank you. That's why the good Lord gives lobsters two claws," he said, continuing to rub it in. "In case you accidentally drop one on the floor, you still have one left to enjoy."

Barbara giggled to herself again, trying to contain the annoying laughter. To distract herself from her embarrassment, she picked up her wine glass and finished the drink. Starting to get a bit tipsy from the white wine, she smiled at him for his generosity. Again the two continued with dinner. Mylok casually refilled her glass and then did the same for himself. Barbara stopped for a few seconds, trying to rest from tackling her two and one-half pound lobster. She took a sip of water for relief. Again, she looked at her date, trying to figure out where he put all his food. Not wanting to waste any food, she returned to her meal.

Mylok coughed a second time. Again, Barbara looked up in concern. His face was a bright red in color. Then, he became very pale in complexion. She blinked hard in disbelief at the look within his eyes. They appeared to be on fire, and his face was alabaster white. He started to have convulsions. He's choking to death, she thought. Barbara screamed for help. The entire room gave attention to her cry. All heads turned toward her. Before anyone knew what was happening, Mylok passed out, his eyes still wide and staring.

Mylok's spirit was lifted from his chair and crucified in midair. His lifeless body remained on the chair. Strange sounds began to enter the large room from all around. Lightning and sparks flew from every point in the room. From within this man came the unseen worlds of heaven and hell. The continuous battle of good and evil was waged around him, but was only seen through the eyes of Mylok's lifted spirit.

Objects started to move on their own. Some even flew across the enormous dining hall. The haunting sight caused many to scream in panic. Many ran as though they were on fire. They pushed their way toward the front door, while others remained motionless in shock. The front door was jammed with customers.

Only known to Mylok was the constant war between angels and demons. His black suit became less noticeable as his spirit began to glow from his eternal energy. The darkly lit room became brighter, as his body became a new light source to him. Deformed spirits rose from the flaming pits of hell. Above were guardian angels defending the gateways to heaven with flaming swords. Hundreds of thousands were seen by Mylok. The restaurant was no longer a reality to him; only a constant battlefield between two separate worlds. An angel spoke to Mylok in an old Latin tongue, while an opposing demon screamed in his ear. No other mortals within the restaurant saw or heard these spirits, for these mortals were blind to this dimension.

Barbara continued to stare at the half dead man, still seated across from her. Slowly, the ghostly paleness passed from Mylok's face as he mysteriously began to breathe again. Things stopped moving, and the unknown sounds slowly left the same way as they had come.

A few of the customers were cut from the flying debris. One man had been stabbed to death through the heart by a steak knife, his wife was mourning his death. Another couple was injured by an over turned table. Some customers were untouched. Nevertheless, the restaurant was demolished. A couple of chandeliers were ripped from the ceiling along with some of the surrounding plaster. Several objects were bent out of shape. One woman stared in disbelief at the many tears in her dress that looked as if they had been done by a tiger's claw.

Barbara soon felt a little pain on her shin. She looked at her leg and noticed that it had been cut by the lobster claw she had dropped on the floor earlier. After untangling the lifeless claw from her pantyhose, she applied pressure to the small gash with a napkin. Barbara then rushed to Mylok's side to help aid in his recovery. She looked at him and asked, "Are you all right?"

As though nothing had happened, Mylok replied, "I couldn't feel better... Maybe we ought to get out of here."

Still in semi-shock, Barbara tugged at his arm to leave the messy establishment. Mylok then pushed his chair back, as he picked up his wine glass. While finishing his unspilled wine, he added, "I bet this is one dinner you won't forget." In the face of such an understatement, Barbara's only response was a slight sigh of relief for the end of this nightmare. As they headed for the door, Mylok put his arm around her for comfort. Realizing that he had forgotten to pay for dinner, Mylok handed the waiter some money. Mylok, being the cause of the disaster, casually said, "Thanks for your services. Keep the change for yourself."

The waiter, while looking at the catastrophe that surrounded him, replied vaguely, "Yeah, thanks." After the couple left through the shattered door, the waiter looked in his palm to see what had been handed to him. He then realized that he held a thousand dollar bill and a cashier's check for one million dollars made payable to the restaurant signed by the First National Bank. An attached note read, "Sorry, hope this covers all the repairs."

On the way to the garage, Barbara stated that she was still too shaken up to drive and thought she would take a cab ride home. Mylok then insisted to drive her home in her car, given her obviously nervous state. They entered the elevator that just so happened to be waiting for them. While inside, Mylok pressed the button for the fourth floor of the seven story garage.

"How did you know my car was on the forth floor?" Barbara asked, knowing that she had not told him.

"A lucky guess," Mylok explained. "The first three floors were full when I entered. I assumed the same was true for you."

The two exited from the elevator and walked down the darkly lit garage. They approached his car first, only to find it being worked over by four street punks. Unable to steal the unique car, they had decided to vandalize it. One hood went to work on the windshield with a baseball bat. Another decided to carve his initials on the door with his car keys. The third vandal was trying to let the air out of the tires with a butterfly knife. None of the three teens were able to make as much as a scratch on Mylok's car. The fourth youth scratched his head, unable to comprehend the lack of damage. A fifth youth was still at work on a Trans Am two cars over. It was obviously a busy night for the gang, because several cars had already been destroyed or partially stripped. The three swore at Mylok's vehicle. Their rage became more violent as they found they were unable to make even the smallest mark on the car. Barbara started to cry as she saw that her car, which happened to be a few cars over from his, had been worked over and spray painted with graffiti. Mylok suddenly tightened his grip around her waist to aid in her support.

Their shadows were soon spotted in the dark garage. A dark bearded face emerged from the gang's van after stealing the hubcaps off another car. He pointed to the couple and yelled at his comrades to take note of them. Mylok, seeing the men working on his car, sarcastically asked them, "Can I help you, gentlemen?"

They laughed in response. Through gritted teeth, the man with the bat said, "Why, is this your car?"

Mylok did not respond. Possibly, he did not want to provoke the men anymore. The four action-seekers approached the couple. The bearded man violently pushed Mylok. Barbara yelled at him to stop the harassment. The hoodlum laughed at her and then started to caress her face, with his buddies harassing her orally as well. Barbara desperately pushed his hand away from her face. Mylok grabbed the hood's hand as he tried to gab Barbara's breast. Barbara moved backward a couple of steps. Unable to move his trapped hand from Mylok's grip, the leader of the vandals decided to swing his free hand toward Mylok's face. He then struck Mylok with great force in the temple area with a devastating hook punch.

Barbara looked on in terror. Most men would have been knocked down by such a blow to the head. Not Mylok! She noticed that he hadn't moved at all. Mylok hadn't even blinked an eye. He just smiled back at the would-be rapist. Then, with the roar of an attacking lion, Mylok threw a damaging kick to the attacker's groin. The hoodlum's love-life quickly ended as he fell to the floor in excruciating pain. Next, a razor sharp knife came slashing at Mylok's midsection. With a lightning quick movement, Mylok blocked the oncoming blade. Two loud sounds echoed in the garage, like hockey sticks breaking in a hockey game. Barbara soon realized that the stabber's elbow and knee had been shattered.

One vandal grabbed Barbara around the waist, pinning her arms to her sides. Then, the hoodlum with the bat figured that he wasn't going to be strike three. He swung at Mylok as a batter would when his team was down one run, with two outs in the final inning. Mylok stepped in and wrapped his arm quickly around his opponent's arms, while also controlling the baseball bat. Like the venomous fangs of a cobra, Mylok's free hand dug in deep into his victim's throat. Strike three! You're out!

The Mark of Zorro was never to be seen. The name writer figured he was not going to leave his initials on this well dressed man. So, dropping his keys to the gang's van, Mr. T-shirt and jeans took off to the nearest exit.

Barbara freed herself by back kicking the grabber in the shin. The man quickly regained his balance on his good leg. Barbara then rushed to Mylok's side for security. With Mylok's eyes searching deep into his soul, the con begged for forgiveness. Mylok felt about as much mercy towards the vandal as the wrongdoer had for Barbara. Nevertheless, the vandal was granted his wish.

With the flames of hell still burning in his eyes, Mylok demanded, "Go! Leave your friends and the van here." Mylok then bent down to pick up the fallen knife, so that the three remaining men would not get any ideas. Two of them appeared to be out cold. The hood that held the knife was still rolling on the cement floor, but he was not going too far on one leg.

Barbara's anger started to turn toward Mylok. "How can you let him get away?" she cried, seeing her totaled car.

In a soft whisper to her, Mylok replied, "I haven't yet." While watching Barbara's assailant limp toward the exit, Mylok tossed the knife upward so that it turned two and a half times in the air. He then caught the blade by the tip. Mylok gave Barbara a soft kiss on the cheek as he swung the knife behind his head. He yelled to the hoodlum, "And this is for Barbara's car!" Mylok threw the knife. The twirling blade flew twenty-five feet across the garage and stuck into the attacker's right buttock.

Barbara's shock led her to step back and trip over the hoodlum's crowbar that laid on the garage floor. With a look of revenge, she looked up at Mylok, and said sarcastically, "Thanks. That just made my night." While in a slight hysterical state of mind concerning the memorable situation, she was offered a hand by Mylok to get back on her feet. Barbara freely accepted his kind offer and fell into his comforting hug. "That was incredible," she said. "How's your eye?"

"I'm fine," Mylok replied. "He barely glazed me."

"Glaze you...I thought that guy was going to kill you."

"It seems that those karate lessons finally paid off."

"I'd say. So, you must be a black belt?" she said excitedly.

"I'm an eclectic martial artist."

"Do you teach?"

"Yes," Mylok replied. "Let me help you to your car." Barbara figured him to be a karate instructor, though she had no intention of taking lessons. With her studies, she neither had the time or the finances.

As they walked toward her car, she noticed that two of the tires on her car had been slashed. "Oh, that's just great. How the hell am I supposed to get home tonight," Barbara said under her breath, knowing she only had one spare tire in the trunk of her car.

"I'll be more than happy to give you a ride home tonight. I'll even call a tow truck for you," Mylok said.

"Thank you. You're much too kind."

"No trouble at all."

Looking at the fallen crumbs, she wondered, "What are we going to do with this low life?"

"Nothing," Mylok replied with a cold smile. "The police can handle it from here."

"They might get away if we call the police," Barbara said. She was worried about the other victims that may come to the garage shortly.

"No need to worry. We'll give the police a call from my car," Mylok said with reassurance, as they walked toward his vehicle.

A phone in his car. This guy must be rich, thought Barbara. As they approached the vehicle, she looked with awe at its unique design. It was metallic silver in color. She noted that the car had no brand name. Shopping for her own car not too long ago, she became aware of many makes and models. Never before had she seen an automobile such as Mylok's. "What make is this?" Barbara asked.

"You could call it a Mylok," he said with a straight face. Figuring that answer would not satisfy her curiosity, he decided also to answer her next predictable question by adding, "I actually designed and built this vehicle."

"You did this?" Barbara asked. "You must be a genius!"

"It's just a model kit car I slapped together," Mylok said modestly. The darkly tinted windows prevented her from observing the interior. Forgetting that the car was probably locked, she instinctively groped for the door handle, only to discover that there was none. Mylok gently pulled her away from the door and gently touched the side of the car. Like magic, the door lifted upward on its own. "How did you do that?" Barbara asked in disbelief.

"A touch sensory unlocking system and a little engineering," Mylok responded.

Figuring that technology wasn't her field of study, she responded, "Oh, I guess that would explain it." Barbara climbed into the front seat and noticed that there was no back seat to the car. That's odd, she thought to herself. Her mind shifted quickly as she sat down, and she saw the dashboard in front of the driver's seat. With so many controls and knobs, it reminded her more of an airplane than a car.

Barbara then saw Mylok through the window about to enter on his side of the car. He's going to have a tough time getting in, she thought, because of the jerk who wedged his car in beside us. Mylok will never get the door to open upward as he did for me. Before her thoughts could wander any farther, the door slid backwards toward the missing trunk. "Well, that's bloody convenient!" Barbara said to Mylok in a sarcastic tone. "Where can I go to get a door like that, so that I can do my grocery shopping?"

Mylok laughed to himself, knowing all the questions she would soon be asking about his car. "Not too many places," he said in answer to her question. Mylok then followed with a few words in a foreign tongue.

"What?" Barbara asked. Figuring he must be speaking his native language to her, she replied with a Spanish accent, "No hablo the Egyptian."

"Sorry, I was just telling my computer to call the police. They'll be here soon," Mylok said.

Figuring that he must be joking, she said to him with a disbelieving look, "Yeah, right!" Mysteriously, the car started up without the use of a key. "Don't tell me, a touch sensory system and a little engineering, right?" Barbara asked as she continued to stare at the magnificent dashboard.

"You got it," Mylok replied. He kept his eyes trained on some device on his dashboard while he began to back the car out of its parking space.

Definitely a unique car, Barbara thought to herself. There was no rear view mirror, nor was there a back window. She noticed a small TV monitor showing the rear view, as the car backed out from the parking spot. She saw the vandal with the broken leg move so that he would not be hit. They drove down four flights in the garage and finally made it to the main street after paying the garage attendant.

Loud sirens could be heard as two police cars screeched around the corner, followed by an ambulance. "That was quick," Barbara stated to Mylok, referring to the telephone call he made before they left. He must have been telling the truth about the computer. What company produces a car like this with such technology? She thought to herself in puzzlement. Believing that if his car looked like this, Mylok's house must also look like a dream, she then had to know about the place where he lived. "So tell me about your place in Bermuda."

"For the time being, I have an apartment not far from here," Mylok said. "How about coming over for a cocktail?"

Barbara thought for a second. Then she figured, Why not? "Sure, I'd like to see your apartment," she said. "I could use another drink after this crazy night."

They finally reached his apartment, number 1402. Barbara had noticed that there were nineteen floors in the elevator, so she no longer expected to see her first penthouse suite. Mylok unlocked the door and swung it open for her. He then flicked on the lights. A rather average one bedroom apartment, she thought to herself. Looked like one large room for combined dining and living. A small kitchenette was off toward the right of the front door. They walked past an oval kitchen table with four chairs around it. Hanging over the table was a light, which reminded her of the lights she'd seen in some tacky bars. On the left wall was a case for a home entertainment center. There were some stereo components and a color TV set.

Mylok held his hand out and made a gesture for her to make herself comfortable on the couch. The couch looked like an old family hand-me-down. It looked to Barbara like one of the old beaten up couches that some of the students brought to their dorm rooms at the university. Well, it must be something to have your own place, Barbara dreamed. It beats having a roommate who keeps you up half the night with her wild parties and drunken boyfriends.

She then noticed the soft music coming from the two corners of the room. It was Barry Manilow--of all people. How did Mylok know that Barry was my favorite singer? She wondered. Barbara listened in a fantasy world. Roo, my 'roomie,' always teases me when I play my Barry Manilow CDs, she thought.

When Barbara entered the room, the call of nature beckoned her. "Where can I go to freshen up?" she asked, needing to make room for another drink.

"Straight ahead," Mylok said while pointing toward a shady, eight foot long hallway. "The light switch is on the inside," he exclaimed as he walked toward the kitchen to prepare a couple drinks for them.

"Thanks!" Barbara replied as she walked toward the bathroom. The door was ajar, so she felt along the inside wall in search of the light switch. Suddenly, she heard a faint scratching sound. Barbara continued to listen as she flicked the bright lights on. Nothing! Probably my imagination, she tried to convince herself, as she started to close the door. Again, she heard the scratching. She slowly opened the bathroom door in hopes of not scaring the noise maker away. She wanted to solve the mystery of the mysterious sound. This time the noise was a little bit more noticeable. Barbara carefully reached for the door handle on her right side. "Oh, I hope it's not a rat," she said under her breath as her heartbeat quickened. She suddenly flung the door open. Barbara jumped back when something came at her. However, it was only the handle of a vacuum cleaner that Mylok had left in the middle of his utility closet.

Barbara grabbed a fresh towel from several others in the closet, now wanting to run warm water on her cool sweat. As she was about to enter the restroom, she heard the scratching again. "God dam!" she said in a low voice, not wanting to go through the ordeal again. Then, realizing what she had said, Barbara shoved the towel in her mouth in hopes Mylok hadn't heard her poor choice of words. Finally, she closed the bathroom door to this strange occurrence.

After she had refreshed herself in the restroom, she opened the door and turned off the lights. The scratching noise continued, but this time it was mingled with a strange animal cry. While standing in the dimly lit hallway, Barbara noticed some light coming from under the door on her right side across from the utility closet. This must be the bedroom of this four room apartment, she figured. Mylok must have shut his cat in the room, somehow knowing I was allergic to them. Strange cry for a cat--or any other animal for that matter, she thought as she opened the bedroom door.

After flicking on the light switch, she realized that it was a rather small bedroom. The neatly made single bed took up most of the room in the middle of the wall next to the bathroom. A large window on the opposite side took up half of that wall. The other half was taken up by a bureau. In the corner next to the window was an extremely cluttered desk. It was obvious that Mylok was extremely busy with something. This was probably how he could afford his unique car, Barbara thought. Partially hidden behind the door on the left was a bookcase. She believed him to be mastering some subject with all the textbooks.

Next to the bookcase was a closet with a sliding door. The lights were coming from there! Again, she heard the cries, which were also coming from the closet. Barbara listened closely to the cry. It sounded as if the creature was trying to say the work "Mylok" repeatedly. The voice sounded almost human, but with a heavy accent. "He must have a talking parrot," she tried to convince herself, as the scratching continued on the other side of the closet door. Barbara reached for the door and was touched by something ice cold on her bare arm. "AHHHH!" she screamed.

"Your drink, Barbara," Mylok said with a grin, anticipating her reaction. "Sorry to have scared you."

A bit outraged by the cruelty to the trapped pet, Barbara asked, "Why did you stick your parrot in the closet?"

"Rooh min hown," (get out of here) Mylok screamed in Arabic at the small beast behind the closet door. A soft scampering slosh was heard, and then all was silent.

"What was that?" Barbara asked in disbelief, as her body shivered from the strange sound. A cold chill went down her spine. It sounded to her like a webbed duck running on a floor of jello. The sloshing noise reminded her of the monster movie, The Beast from the Swamp Lands, she had seen as a young girl.

"Just a pet," Mylok said. "The apartment complex doesn't allow animals in the building, so I have to keep him behind the closet door."

"Can I see him?" Barbara pleaded.

"Sorry," Mylok said while shaking his head. "He's gone."

"Oh come on! Where can he go in a closet?" Barbara asked as she started to slide the door back.

Mylok gently grabbed her hand and looked into her eyes. "Things are not always what they seem. Forget about it," he said to Barbara. "Come. Let's enjoy our drinks." He handed her an exotic frozen creation, and then picked up his drink from the bookcase where he had placed it a few seconds before.

They both started for the living room. Barbara could still hear the music in the background. As Mylok turned his back to exit through the bedroom door, Barbara's curiosity became too much to handle. She just had to see Mylok's pet. Against her better judgment, she quickly slid the door backward. "What the..." Inside the closet was another doorway leading into a different room.

Two seven foot tall metallic rods were positioned in the middle of the closet floor. These rods became the outside door frames of a door leading to another way of life. She entered the closet to have a better view of the palace-sized room. Many enormous statues carved from stone were along the walls. It looked to Barbara like ancient Egyptian architecture. Thousands of drawings and hieroglyphics were carved into the enormous walls. The ceiling changed shades of orange and red. It was alive and active like the blue sky she remembered that morning, but only in different colors.

Mylok, enraged by her action, shattered the glass in his very hand. His orange, pineapple, and cherry fell to the floor as glass flew across his bedroom from the extreme pressure Mylok exerted on it. Knowing what had happened, Mylok shook his head and then turned to walk towards Barbara. Mylok was neither cut nor drenched by the full drink. A piece of glass was driven half way into the wall as the yellow and green frozen cocktail continued to drip from his bedroom ceiling.

Barbara's hand disappeared as it passed through the platinum doorway. She quickly pulled it back to examine it. "I must be dreaming," she muttered to herself.

"I suppose you would like me to pinch you to see if you're dreaming," a voice responded over her shoulder.

"Ouch," Barbara said as Mylok pinched her on the butt.

"All right, so I'm not dreaming. What is this place?" Knowing now the configuration of his apartment, she added, "It sure isn't your living room." Barbara knew that such a door had to lead into his living room, if not to a fourteen story drop.

With a mesmerizing look, Mylok answered her in a Rod Serling voice, "You're about to enter another dimension. Not only a dimension of sight and sound, but of mind. Your next stop..." Then in his normal voice, he finished, "My real home." He held her around the waist for support, lest she faint. "Some technology seems to surpass reason at times. Only a few years ago man set foot on the moon. A short time before that, it was considered an impossible task. Do you see, Barbara? You must now empty your mind, so that you can fill it with new ideas."

Still in a complete daze, Barbara said, "Sure I understand that, but that doesn't explain this or the car you drive...or how you beat up those guys so easily." She glanced to the right for a split second at the lack of clothes in his closet. Outright, she added, "You work for the FBI or something?"

"No, I don't work for the FBI. You will find it hard to believe at first, but in time you will understand everything you wish to know." While holding her close, Mylok continued to gauge her response as they stepped through the doorway. "Welcome to the Bermuda Triangle."

"Ha ha. Very funny. How is it possible to travel one thousand miles in less than a second?" Barbara replied in a half-believing voice.

"Tsk tsk," Mylok said. "You mustn't close your mind. You told me yourself that this is not my living room."

"But, how?"

"Remember a few seconds ago when you thought your hand disappeared?" Mylok reminded her.

"Yeah..."

"In a sense, it did vanish as it traveled into a different dimensional location." Seeing her skepticism, Mylok continued, "Like a TV set receiving a transmitted signal, so too, can this door passage transmit and receive the molecular structure of a living being." Mylok smiled at Barbara, while she continued to look at him as if he were somewhat insane. "If you don't believe me, try putting your hand through the door again." Seeing the terrified look in her eyes, Mylok said encouragingly, "Go ahead. It won't bite. You already made it through in one piece. Right?"

Barbara, believing that she was still dreaming, decided to accompany her fantasy. The huge room was dead silent except for the Barry Manilow CD still playing in the background. Barbara looked at the familiar bedroom through the doorway. However, instead of metallic rods supporting the door, she found some Egyptian wall carvings. A pair of twenty foot bird/men stone statues mirrored each other on the right and left sides of the bedroom's doorway. She slowly placed her finger through the opening and it vanished. "That's neat! I don't feel anything," Barbara said as she looked at him. "But why does it disappear like that?"

"Because it's no longer here. It's back at the apartment. Go ahead and walk through it, if you like. You'll still be able to see me," Mylok said, trying to gain her faith in him.

While only seeing the bedroom ahead of her, Barbara slowly walked through and noted no change. Then, she turned and saw Mylok standing in the same spot. He looked out of place to Barbara--standing there in a three piece suit among Egyptian artifacts. Strange, though, there was no sign of deterioration within the colossal room, she noted to herself.

Mylok gesture for her to return to him. "Come. I have a lot more to show you if you wish," he said with enthusiasm.

"Oh yes, please do!" Barbara said with excitement, as she walked back to him. "How did you get this?"

"It wasn't from winning any lottery," he said jokingly. "Remember a few years ago when you were camping and you had the alien encounter?" Mylok asked, reminding her of the day she saw a UFO and believed she had seen two extraterrestrial life forms.

"How do you know about that?" Barbara asked, shocked by his words. "I've never told anyone about that day, fearing they wouldn't believe me." Since she was the only one who had experienced the encounter, she tried for many years to convince herself that it had not really happened at all. That was why she was now studying astronomy in college and learning about extraterrestrial intelligence. "You're that man with those two aliens I saw!" she shouted hysterically.

"Yes, I am," he said softly, hoping to ease her anxiety.

Barbara knew that Mylok had saved her life. They met by accident. While hiking in the woods with some of her friends, Barbara had become separated from the group. After climbing up a mountain, the girls were returning to their campground. While walking single file behind the other girls, Barbara thought it would be fun to beat the other girls back to the campsite. It was her understanding that cutting off the path then would be a shortcut back. Unfortunately, Barbara's practical joke turned into a nightmare. She quickly got lost in the dense forest. Night fell quickly. She spotted some lights in the distance. Believing them to be lights from her campsite, she walked toward them.

Instead, she came upon what she believed to be a UFO. It was saucer shaped on the bottom, however cupped on the top. Several windows circled around the top of the space ship, and there was a high pitched humming sound. Many bright lights and steam radiated from the craft. Shocked by the strange sight, she let a man who she now realized was Mylok lead her back to the proper path. Barbara believed that if it hadn't been for him, she might have died from starvation, if not from exposure to the cold night air. That whole night was still a blur to her. "I guess I owe you my life," Barbara said. "Thank you."

Mylok knew she would have died. She was heading away from her camp and civilization. He could not let the young girl die! "Let me assure you that I'm a human being just like yourself," he said to her. "When I was seventeen years of age, I was abducted by aliens from a different world. For many years they taught me to use my mind to its limits. As you know, today's modern man uses less than ten percent of his brain's capability. These aliens showed me how to maximize over eighty-five percent of my existing mind. With their knowledge, there's nothing that I don't already know or can't learn. Barbara, I've known you since your grandfather's death. His past is very important to me."

"My grandfather?" Barbara said confused, knowing that he must be taking about her late father's father. Her other grandfather was very much alive in a nursing home.

"What can you tell me of him?"

"Not much, I'm afraid. I was about seven years old when he died of a heart attack," Barbara said. The trip to Chicago lasted less than a week, she recalled. After which, she flew to Kansas to visit her relatives on her uncle Cal's cattle ranch. Auntie Rose told her of her grandfather's tragic death a few days into her visit. That short week was the only time she had to spend with her grandfather. At age seven, she was more into play, not socializing. "I barely knew him."

"What do you know of his profession?" Mylok asked. He knew her grandfather's death was a result from more than just a heart attack.

"I believe he was an archaeologist?"

"He was," Mylok said. "Do you know of his trip to Tibet?"

"Tibet? I never knew that." Barbara mused. "I believe that was twelve years ago. What do you care? How do you know these things?"

"Come," Mylok said. "I'll show you how it's done and answer all your questions."

"In there."

"I have no intention of hurting you, Barbara," Mylok said. "Trust your feelings. You know that seeing is believing."

"Yes, I'd like to know everything," Barbara said as they walked toward what seemed to be the front of an Egyptian temple. Huge columns rose about forty feet high with stairs leading to two Sphinx statures guarding a small entrance. The walk seemed to be endless as Barbara believed the room to be a bit larger than a football field. She noticed that the many stone statues seemed to move, as the changing red glow from above varied its intensity, therefore casting different shadows. Yet, she still knew that they were lifeless rock. Barbara then said in a harsh tone, "You did say that we're on the Bermuda Triangle. Which island are we supposedly on, then?"

"We're on no island..."

Before he could finish, Barbara jumped in, "Then we're on a ship?"

"No. We're miles beneath the Atlantic Ocean and we're also below the earth's crust," Mylok explained while pointing to the now orange sky above. "Those lights above are actually molten lava."

As a five year old child would taunt a fellow sibling, Barbara replied, "Oh yeah? Then how come it doesn't come pouring down on us?"

"Again, you have closed your mind," Mylok reprimanded her. "Think before you speak! What transparent substance lets light through, but keeps the elements out?"

"Glass?" she replied in answer to his riddle.

"Right. However, normal glass would melt under such extreme heat. Also, the intense light would be like looking at the sun. It would make us go blind. Instead, we used a tinted crystal dome to aid our need."

Unable to forget the lava overhead, she barely heard his last words. She said, "Well, it's a neat effect anyway." Barbara then looked up at the many stairs they now had to climb. The guarded entrance was a lot bigger than she expected. It seemed to have tripled in size while she had been talking to Mylok. Her high heeled shoes started to become unbearable. At the bottom of the stairs, she sat down to rest her aching feet.

Mylok then saw how tired she was becoming. It was a long night for anyone, except for him. Nevertheless, he decided not to let her stop yet. "Almost there! You can't stop now. Why don't you take your shoes off if they bother you so much? Must be practical." As he removed his jacket and vest to help her feel more relaxed, he added, "You can leave them here for now. We'll get them later." As she was removing her second shoe, Mylok turned his back and bent down to offer her a "piggy-back" ride up the stairs. "Hop on! I'll carry you up."

Barbara was not going to refuse this gallant gesture, so she said, "All right!" Mylok's position reminded her of the horseback riding days, while visiting her uncle's cattle ranch in Kansas. Barbara's died father's sister married a rancher's son. As Barbara mounted Mylok like a horse, she wrapped her left arm around his neck and with her free hand slapped him on the butt. She hollered, "Giddy-up!" Like a proud black and white stallion, Mylok galloped up the many stairs at full stride. Barbara held on for dear life in hopes she would not fall off. They finally reached the top of the stairs and Barbara hollered, "Whoa!" She gave him a little kiss on the cheek and patted him on the head as she dismounted. "Nice horsy," she said.

Mylok turned around and looked at her. He figured her childish behavior deserved more of the same. While shaking his head, he neighed like a tired horse.

Barbara started to laugh as she got the hint of her behavior and wiped the spittle off her face. She figured he must be in great shape because he was not even breathing hard, nor had he worked up a sweat. Barbara looked back to see where they had come from. With so many other openings, it was hard to tell which entrance they had used. The stone floor was rather comfortable to her stocking feet, as was the temperature in the enormous room. The lava light ceiling did not at all cause any discomfort from the firing lights. She then jokingly exclaimed to Mylok, "With a ceiling like that, I bet you have no heating bills."

"True. However, you can't imagine our bills for air conditioning."

At first, Barbara only gave him a dirty stare for topping her sense of humor so quickly. Then, she chuckled at his clever reply. The once tiny door now towered over them twenty feet as they approached its entrance. As they walked down a long hall, Barbara glanced at the unusual symbols on the large walls and tried to decipher their meaning. She figured them to be Egyptian hieroglyphics from pictures she had seen in a few of her anthropology textbooks. "Can you read this?" she asked.

"Oh yes, every word of it. It tells of my life's story," Mylok said as his hand pointed to some colorful carvings along the wall.

Barbara was still in a state of disbelief, as she looked at the many different murals along the wall. They passed one carving of thousands of men apparently cultivating fields of crops. Another one showed a close up of a man with great terror in his expression as he looked over his shoulder at an enormous sun reaching several feet high to the solid stone ceiling above. Barbara thought the walls were about twenty-five feet away from her on both sides. The ceiling also seemed to be fifty feet high, therefore forming a square. The hall seemed to go on for about a quarter of a mile, but her excitement kept her going without any pain. They soon approached a great shrine cut deep into the massive stone walls.

Barbara looked at another carved mural. This one was a close-up of a young man holding a dying man close to him while others continued to work in an empty field. A tear came to Barbara's eye as she realized the young man greatly resembled Mylok. Now realizing that the pyramid shaped shrine was really a tomb, Barbara asked in a sorrowful tone, "Was that your father?"

"It's in memory of him. If it wasn't for him, I wouldn't be here today," Mylok said as he looked at the massive slab of stone. He gently tugged at her hand to continue their journey. "Not there yet."

Again they continued to walk. Barbara saw a figure standing alone in a massive lightning storm carved in still more rock. Again, they passed another statue. Barbara was caught off guard at this unusually shaped stone statue, for she was too busy looking at the colorful pictures carved in the wall. "Yuck," she said in a low voice about the statue. The head of the statue was malformed. The cranium was definitely too large for the rest of the statue's body. Barbara was startled by this strange statue of a hairless man, who had six fingers on each of his hands.

"Have some respect," Mylok said with amusement at Barbara's reaction. "He's a good friend of mine. This alien saved my life and gave me his wisdom."

"Then you're saying that there is alien life."

"Of course. With these billions of stars in the universe, many with planets around them like our earth, it's a bit naive to think that we're the only living civilization among the heavens," Mylok said.

"Then that really was a UFO I saw that night when I was camping. Those other two with you were actually aliens?" Barbara asked him.

"Yes," Mylok replied. "You saw them with your own eyes."

Barbara stared at the statue as they passed through the doorway leading to another massive room. However, this room was only the size of her aunt and uncle's Colonial house. It was a barren room with a thirty foot golden cross in the middle. The ends of the cross came to tapered, sharp points. She wondered how it could stay upright without tipping over. Wrapped around it was a vivid lifelike dragon.

"Come. It won't hurt you as long as you're with me," Mylok said.

Of course not, thought Barbara, as they traveled toward a door at the opposite side of the room. How could a statue hurt you; unless of course, it toppled over on top of them due to the precarious balance of the cross? When they entered the room, she noticed a wretched stench in the air. The eyes of the dragon seemed to follow them as they walked under the massive statue. It looked as if the head moved slightly with them. It must be an optical illusion, she thought.

Her attention was then caught by another doorway approximately thirty feet from the doorway they were heading toward, on the same wall at the far side. Strange stone carvings of angels, cupids, and ugly looking demons were around the door. Their bodies were all intertwined with one another. It looked to Barbara like the creatures were engaged in a rumble; or possibly, Mylok had a strange sense of humor for an orgy.

As they were about to enter another hall, she had the feeling they were not alone. Barbara turned her head and again looked at the statue. She gasped a little at the strange sight. The cross had turned completely around on its axis, and still looking at them was the dragon. This time, Barbara knew the dragon to be in an entirely different position. "It's alive!" Barbara shrieked as she held Mylok's arm tightly.

"Yes, it's alive. No need to worry. It won't harm you as long as it knows you're with me."

"I thought there was no such thing as dragons," Barbara stuttered.

"Many of your legends came from reality, Barbara," Mylok went on. "Unfortunately, knights, wizards, and the like made them extinct just like the once mighty buffalo and the dodo bird. They killed the dragons as game and food. This is the last of them."

"I thought they all had wings," she said, looking at the wingless beast and remembering the flying dragons of Chinese origin.

"There were once many different species of dragons. Some species had wings," Mylok said.

Barbara didn't bother asking her next question, feeling that it was too stupid to ask. She once remembered a movie where a sorcerer had to be present whenever a dragon was alive. Well, she thought to herself, you cannot believe everything you see in the movies.

They soon approached another doorway. There, Mylok touched an ever changing circle of colors about the size of his hand on the side of the passage. Barbara watched over his shoulder and saw, or thought she saw, the room suddenly change in size and design. Having had only a quick glimpse first, she concluded that the late hour and alcohol were playing tricks with her eyes. To save herself from embarrassment, she decided not to mention anything.

The enormous room looked to be from about the year 3000. The size of the room reminded her of a furnished Colonial house without the walls to divide the separate rooms. The room stood two stories high. It was covered with chrome walls, gold inlay and marble pillars. It was quite a change from the old Egyptian architecture. The new room was about the same size as the one with the dragon. However, some of the furniture seemed to have no value or purpose to Barbara, though it appeared to be highly technical. She stared in awe, unable to believe its unique design.

"What do you think?" Mylok asked as he motioned for her to be seated on an oversized couch.

"It's fabulous!" Barbara said. While massaging her foot, she noted strange music coming from all around. Yet, she could not detect any speakers. The music at least fits the room, she thought to herself. It's certainly unique. Barbara followed Mylok to the right side of the room. Mylok then sat her behind three large computer monitors. He was obviously very busy with some engineering problem. There was no apparent keyboard, so Barbara felt pleased that she would not have to rely on her poor typing skills. She stared at the oversized CRT in front of her. "Great! If I understood hieroglyphics, I might even be able to help you out," Barbara moaned.

"Oh ye of little faith!" Then, Mylok chanted something seemingly in Egyptian, and the screen changed. Barbara than saw a movie on the central screen of an American within an ancient chamber. "Do you recognize him?"

"Is that my grandfather?"

"Yes," Mylok said. "He's within the Temple of the Holy Golden Dragon. This hidden Tibetan temple was the holiest monastery in the world until your grandfather's archaeological discovery."

"What did he find?"

"Your grandfather disturbed and had taken an artifact of unearthly powers," Mylok explained. "If not returned quickly to it's proper place, this artifact will bring great destruction to the earth."

"I might have known," Barbara said in disbelief. "It's always the end of the world when the priceless item is stolen."

"This is no joke, Barbara," Mylok screamed, slamming the table in front of her. Barbara jumped in her sit. "This artifact is not of this world. Your grandfather is the key to the earth's survival. It is no coincidence that your grandfather died on Saturday, April 26, 1986. The same day the great nuclear disaster of Chernobyl, Ukraine, occurred."

"You expect me to believe that the removal of this artifact, in Tibet, led to the death of thousands of people, on the other side of Russia I might add, as well as my grandfather," Barbara stated, as she shock her head in disgust of such an alleged fabrication.

"Yes," Mylok said. "As hard as it is to believe, it is the truth."

"As I told you before, I hardly knew the man!" Barbara exclaimed, referring to her grandfather. "Why are you doing this to me? I don't have anything else to tell you." She truly believed that. Barbara never even knew her grandfather's home address. Only that he lived somewhere near Chicago.

"Without that artifact, your world is at great risk," Mylok said sadly. "I'm sorry to have put you threw this."

Barbara could not believe his story. How could she be in the Bermuda Triangle? Her grandfather? The Chernobyl disaster? Could this be some elaborate hoax? Possibly a con to get his hands on her grandfather's priceless artifact? Her head raced with ideas. After relaxing for a short time, she finally came down from her excitement and returned to reality. It was getting late. Barbara had to get back to the university to study for her final exam in French.

She had been required to take an elective in language. It had come down to a choice between French or British Literature. French seemed to be more fun at the time. Unfortunately, she received a "D" on her mid-term exam. Due to work on her major courses, she had to neglect her studies in French. She had never before received a grade below a "B." However, waitressing really took a lot out of her. Getting a lousy grade in French would hurt her grade point average and maybe even her scholarship. Now, in a state of mild panic, Barbara turned to Mylok and said, "I'm sorry, but I have to go home to study for a final exam in French. Do you know what time it is?"

"It's 2:07," Mylok responded without the aid of a clock or watch. "If you would like, I can tutor you. It just so happens that I speak French like a native."

"Thanks, I appreciate that," Barbara said. "Unfortunately, I don't have my textbook or notes. I'll still have to go home to get them."

"You don't need them," Mylok exclaimed. "All textbooks teach the same fundamentals of the language. This computer can teach you the same thing. By the time you went home and then to class, you would have wasted an hour that you could have used for studying."

"To tell you the truth, I haven't really studied this whole semester due to my other work. It wouldn't even be worth it," she groaned, while giving up hope of even passing the course. She had lost her motivation primarily due to her loss of sleep the past few nights because of her other work and studying. She planned to retake French the following fall. This was one of the reasons why Barbara was willing to go out on the date with Mylok in the first place.

"Nonsense! You just need a good motivator," Mylok said with reassurance.

Barbara was feeling tired from the long night and did not wish to waste Mylok's time studying for an exam she knew she was going to fail anyway. It seemed that the course would just have to be retaken next semester. Mylok chanted a few words in what sounded to be Egyptian and the monitor changed into an English/French translation.

The monitor reminded Barbara of the first page of her textbook. Maybe it will work after all, she thought. Half of her exam was to be oral and the other half written. After a few minutes, all the screens were covered with material from her French class. All the verbs she had trouble with were placed on the left screen so that she could go back to them as needed. Quickly, she learned the spelling and pronunciations of the words. As she did, they were deleted from the screen and new words were added.

A couple of hours passed as she responded to Mylok's sentences in French. While he continued to stand over her, Mylok would aid Barbara in her replies. The table in front of them also had a glass covered screen.

This screen gave her many questions and problems to solve. Barbara held a special metallic pen which enabled her to write on the screen like paper. Mylok would praise her when she was right and would playfully tease her when she made a mistake. His help made it fun for her to learn increasingly. Occasionally, the computer would repeat the same problem to verify that she had actually learned it. After four hours of study, Barbara had learned more about French than she had the entire semester.

"It's 6:15," Mylok told Barbara. "It's been a long night. You should get some rest before your exam."

Her exam was at 8:20 in the morning; only two hours away. However, the intense studying made her too excited to sleep. "I'm not tired. Please, let's continue with the studying," she pleaded, feeling now that there was hope of passing her final exam.

"You must sharpen your ax!" Mylok exclaimed.

"What is that supposed to mean?"

"A lumberjack needs a sharp ax to make his work easy, like you need a sharp and relaxed mind for your exam," Mylok told Barbara. "You wouldn't want to fall asleep in the middle of your final."

"I guess you're right. But, I'm too hyper to sleep."

"Let's go. You can rest on my bed," Mylok insisted.

Barbara felt somewhat confident with what she had learned. At least now I have a chance of passing the final exam, she thought to herself. After finishing her doodle of a smiley-face on the exam screen, she pushed the chair back and followed Mylok past a luxurious couch. "I don't want to kick you out of your bed. I'll be glad to sleep on the couch," Barbara stated.

"I insist."

They continued to walk toward the far wall of the Colonial house sized room. Barbara stared at what she believed to be a fabulous underwater painting. It must have been ten feet high and forty feet across. As she approached the "mural," she saw movement of some of the ocean plants. Only then did Barbara realize that this was a window to the under sea world. In the lower left of the window, was the largest octopus that she had ever seen.

Mylok then turned to her and showed her his bed. "Enjoy your rest," he said.

Barbara first looked at the bed, believing it to be an oversized table. There was no mattress! "You have a bad back or something?" she asked. This must be a poor joke, she thought. Barbara exclaimed, "I think I'd enjoy the couch better."

"Fine," Mylok said as he threw his body onto the bed so that he would land on his back. However, his body never touched the surface. Instead, he floated on an invisible energy field. His body was a foot above its surface. Mylok then placed his hands behind his head and grinned at Barbara. He added, "You don't know what you're missing. It's like sleeping on a cloud."

"That looks like fun. Can I try it?" Barbara pleaded with enthusiasm.

"I already gave you a chance and you blew it, kid," Mylok said, as he started to close his eyes, trying to provoke some reaction. "If you want to try it, now you're going to have to fight me for it."

"All right, if you insist," she said. Her desire to try the bed led her to dive on top of poor Mylok and wrestle him for it. Barbara tugged on his arm to try to throw him off of the energy field bed. Due to the alcohol she had that night, and the many times she had wrestled with her boyfriend, Paul, she attacked Mylok out of pure instinct and habit. Barbara and Paul would wrestle just for the fun of it while watching boring TV shows. Often, they would also engage in pillow fights.

Shortly, Mylok gave in graciously and let her take over. She then placed her hands behind her head as he had done before and grinned back at him. "You're right. It's like floating on a cloud," Barbara said.

Mylok was not going to let her get the best of him. "Would you believe, it's adjustable too," Mylok said with a vengeful tone. At the same time he reached for a domed shape object at the foot of the "bed." While holding his hand over the dome, he raised and lowered his hand many times. This action caused the energy field in the bed to increase and decrease, thus, tossing Barbara into the air several times. As on a trampoline, she screamed with excitement.

Barbara then rolled over onto her side. With her finger, she tried to poke a hole through the energy field and touch the solid surface beneath. However, she could not. The force field was too strong. The energy source felt kind of like a rubber ball to her. The harder she pressed, the more it would resist. She was still a foot from the hard surface. Soon, she stood up on the invisible trampoline and noted almost no change. Still, she could not touch the surface of the table. Barbara then started jumping up and down like a young child on its parents' king-size bed.

Mylok just watched with amusement. He then screamed at her, "Hey! Do you want to break the springs?"

Barbara looked up at him after staring at the hard surface under her stocking feet through the invisible field. She plopped down into a sitting position. Concerned that she had done the bed some damage, she said, "I'm terribly sorry." Barbara then thought to herself, There were no springs to break. Seeing the hint of a smile beginning to break out on Mylok's face, she knew that he was only joking. Barbara then giggled at her foolish action.

"Time to get some rest," Mylok said.

Barbara laid back on the bed. She could now feel how tired she was from the long night. However, her adrenalin was still up and her breathing and heartbeat were still accelerated from all the exercise. She started to break out in a sweat. Too restless to sleep now, she thought, as she looked at the octopus through the ocean window on her left. A shudder ran down her spine. After seeing the movie "Jaws," she was never at ease being near an ocean.

Mylok knew that she needed to rest, if she were to do well on her French exam. Holding his hand over her eyes, he softly told her, "Relax."

With her mind wandering, Barbara responded, "This bed won't wrinkle my dress, will it?"

"Shhhhh. Twenty minutes of self-hypnosis can be worth eight hours of regular sleep," Mylok said in a soft voice. He continued, "Close your eyes and empty your mind of any thoughts. Just let them drift away... Now take a deep breath. As you did in your mother's womb, breathe with your abdomen not your upper chest. Hold...Exhale. Again, inhale. Hold... Exhale. Good, keep breathing like that. Imagine your body to be a bottle. Someone has just pulled the cork out of your belly button. Let all tension pour out of your body as you exhale..." After a few more deep breaths, she was sound asleep. Mylok gently kissed her on the forehead and left her so that she could enjoy her rest.

While Barbara rested, Mylok went to a conference room with twenty-one of his top scientists--each a master in his own field. The huge room contained a sunken floor which sat the scientists in a horseshoe pattern.

Above the sunken area were three large TV monitors for the research development. At the open end of the horseshoe, on top of nine stairs, Mylok was positioned behind a platform with an extensive control panel.

A scientist touched his heart then head and extended his hand toward his Pharaoh, saying in his native tongue, "Mylok, as foreseen in your writings of the ages, outside man has forsaken our warnings and taken two of our orbs. Without our light of guidance, the end of the earth is imminent."

"Yes," Mylok said while pointing out the monitors overhead. "The Orb of Sun-God Ra must be returned before it's too late. It must be returned to us before greater harm is done. Its powers are far too great! Nevertheless, without the second orb in our possession, the value of the third orb is meaningless. Therefore, I must make a quest for the return of the second orb."

"My heart goes with you," the twenty-one scientists and priests said together as a blessed farewell for success. As Mylok bowed his head for their blessing, they left the conference room in two rows around Mylok's platform.

"Give this to Maxalavar," said Mylok in his native language to his secretary. With his left hand upon his friend's shoulder, Mylok handed a small device to the man. "Have him wake up Barbara. Send her to me in the Room of Souls."

half hour later, Barbara was awakened
by a feeling of pressure on her chest.
Still dazed, it felt to her as if someone
was gently shaking her midsection with two hands. Still in a state of
semiconsciousness, it also seemed to her that a third hand was trying to
go between her legs. She was now dimly aware of a chanting of the word
"Mylok." The voice was familiar. Barbara moaned, desperately wanting
to hold onto her "rest of the dead," but she was forced to open her eyes.
She then saw a blue eyed face staring back at her. It was not Mylok! Afraid
the creature would invade her body, she threw it to the floor. Barbara
screamed as if she were being raped. She then looked toward the floor to
see a hideous dwarf rolling in pain.

The creature finally was able to stand up. It looked to be about two
feet tall. The human looking face again smiled back at her after first
moving its head back and forth a few times to shake off the pain of
bumping it. The mutant beast had its black hair tied back into a foot long
braid. The green beast had the body of a giant scaly tadpole with white
scales going down its spine. Though the creature had no hands, it was
able to keep itself upright because of its two muscular legs and its long
prehensile tail. The tiny monster brought its tail over his head to point at
an object placed at the foot of the energy field bed. Again the happy face
said the word, "Mylok."

Barbara looked at the small object. She did not recall it being there
before. Barbara believed that Mylok had left it there for her. It looked first

to be a hand held calculator. Barbara looked closely at the object to see a set pattern of flickering lights that formed an arrow. Barbara then figured that this small box was going to take her to Mylok. After turning to look back toward the creature, Barbara said, "Thank you."

While balancing on its frog like feet, the creature saluted back to her with his tail, indicating its mission had been accomplished. As she looked away to peer again at the object on the table, the creature quietly jumped over the couch to hide from her. Being thrown to the floor, the wise beast suddenly became self-conscious of its ugly appearance after scaring the beauty, Barbara.

However, Barbara believed the shy creature had apparently run away. While sitting up on the energy field bed, she looked around the room. She looked down at the floor to see her shoes placed neatly at the foot of the "bed." She gracefully slipped them on her feet. After grabbing the pointer from the table, she started to walk, following the arrow's direction. Barbara purposely turned her body several times, but the pointer always pointed toward the exit door (the only door) through which she had previously entered just a few hours ago. She walked slowly past the couch. With her attention focused on the small device that she held, Barbara was unaware of the beast hiding behind the couch.

The lonely frog/man gazed at the back of Barbara's dress as she unknowingly walked past. Pleased with the beautiful sight, the creature raised his eyebrows a couple of times. While continuing to watch Barbara's cute fanny wiggle away through her tight, light green dress, the deformed dwarf lustfully licked his lips.

Barbara walked toward the exit. She first feared that the pointer would never lead her to Mylok. It was pointing toward the hallway wall. Once she entered the hallway, however, the pointer suddenly pointed to the right. As she turned, it again pointed straight.

It soon led her back to the room with the golden cross. Barbara peeped around the corner to see the dragon roaming around the room. Fear coursed through her body. The wide hallway was probably large enough for the dragon to pursue her. At this moment, Barbara hoped that the dragon did not eat meat. If it did, her only hope was that Mylok kept the dragon well fed. As the dragon turned to face her, Barbara screamed, "Don't hurt me! I'm with Mylok!" Uninterested in her words, the dragon sought comfort on the cross. Again, the dragon stared back at Barbara, while perching over her twenty feet in the center of the huge room.

Barbara felt like a goddess, believing her words could control such a destructive monster. Filled with new found power, she teasingly said, "You wimp."

The bored dragon then gave a timely yawn. It bared its razor sharp teeth to Barbara, and its yawn sounded like a roar to her.

"Just kidding!" Barbara tried to convince the dragon, now believing that she was going to be eaten alive. With her back pressed to the wall, she slowly lifted her hand to check the direction of the arrow. Not taking her eyes off the dragon, she saw the arrow point along the wall. While hugging the wall tightly with her back, Barbara slowly shuffled toward the door with the spiritual carvings. Again, she glanced at the arrow. This time it was pointing behind her. Barbara walked backward through the smaller doorway. She now felt safe from the dragon. Barbara heard foreign words being spoken behind her. She quickly turned when she recognized Mylok's voice.

"Mylok!" Barbara cried out. She saw the back of Mylok; he was dressed in a white Egyptian priest's robe. Around his neck was a wide gold necklace. Many long tapering strips of gold were fastened together with tiny gold rings. It reminded Barbara of ancient Egyptian priests from pictures in her old textbooks.

Mylok was kneeling down in front of two vertical energy fields. Within the fields were his two opposing entities. On the left side was a rather handsome looking transparent spirit. This angel looked to be the mightiest of warriors. On the right side was a demon having the body of half a goat and bat-like wings. Barbara thought him to be the devil himself. Both of the spirits shot back into Mylok's chest, entering his soul. Mylok turned around to see a catatonic Barbara. Her eyes were open wide--unbelieving of what she had just seen.

"What were they?" Barbara asked in shock.

"It is what it appeared to be, Barbara," Mylok replied.

"They looked like ghosts."

"Two conflicting entities are the essence of every man's soul," Mylok said. "It is these spirits that teach you right from wrong. Every time you speak to yourself, you are speaking to your soul spirits. Only in death, is one entity consumed by the other." Mylok figured that she did not need to be thinking of these things during her final exam, so he quickly changed the subject. He continued, "I see that Maxalavar finally woke you up. Did you enjoy your rest?"

"Yes, thank you," Barbara finally responded after a long pause from the shock. "What was that thing that woke me up? It looked like the creation of a mad scientist," Barbara said, referring to Mylok's half man and half dragon pet.

"Maxalavar was an experiment of a cellular reconstruc-tion," Mylok explained.

"It scared the daylights out of me," Barbara said with a chill running down her spine. "It's hideous."

"I wouldn't tell him that to his face. Maxalavar is extremely intelligent and very sensitive about his looks."

"He does have a cute smile and beautiful blue eyes. His balding black hair reminds me of my uncle Cal," Barbara said in an attempt to make up for her previous remarks.

"You should tell Maxalavar that some time."

Barbara chilled again at the thought of that. "I think that I may have hurt him when I threw him out of bed," Barbara said in a sorrowful tone. "He ran off before I could tell him how sorry I was."

"Don't worry about it. He's shy when it comes to strangers," Mylok said to ease her tension. He added jokingly, "You don't have to worry about hurting him. He has a hard head." Again, he diverted her attention toward the approaching French exam. "At least Maxalavar could pass your exam in French, if he wanted to," Mylok said. "Maxalavar has an IQ of 182."

"Are you kidding?"

"No." After her long night, Mylok knew Barbara needed a quick breakfast for energy to do well on the final. "Time to get a quick bite to eat before your exam," Mylok exclaimed.

"Right...I must sharpen my ax!"

Amused that she had remembered his exact words, he added with a slight chuckle, "Good, you're now beginning to open your mind. Come. I'll take you to the university."

"You're not going to take me dressed like that, are you?" Barbara asked, concerned that they might be spotted by some of her classmates.

"No," Mylok said as he removed the necklace and robe. Underneath, he wore a different pair of black slacks, without the pin-striping, and a colorful shirt.

"Whoa! Pull the plug on that shirt," she said.

"I take it you don't like the shirt."

"Nobody wears a shirt like that," Barbara tried to convince him.

"At least not in your part of the world," Mylok said, hinting at a surprise he had for Barbara. "It is time that we leave for the university," he said holding his hand out to lead her toward a mirror like doorway. Before her eyes, the door led to his apartment's closet.

Like a TV transmission signal, Mylok's doorway was able to lead him anywhere in his world. Mylok's telepathic mind enabled him to signal the door to its new location. However, this was only possible due to the hundreds of years spent with his alien friends.

Barbara figured, if it was possible to travel over a thousand miles by walking through a doorway, anything was possible for Mylok. As they entered his shabby apartment, Barbara noticed that she had about an hour before the exam. Mylok offered her a quick shower as he began to prepare a fast breakfast for the two of them. As she was about to close the bathroom door, she turned to thank him. "Thanks for walking back and getting my shoes this morning. I know it's quite a trip back there."

"You can thank Maxalavar for that," he said, as he walked toward the kitchen to prepare breakfast.

Once in the shower, she vigorously scrubbed her body with a new bar of soap, which was still in its original wrapper and placed in the soap dish for her. It felt good to her to get rid of the sticky feeling after a long night of dancing. She did not bother with washing her hair due to the lack of time. After her refreshing shower, Barbara opened the curtain and searched for a towel. A fresh one had been placed on the towel rack. The towel she used last night had been taken away. Mylok must have some maid service, she thought to herself.

Walking into the living room, Barbara could smell the food cooking in the kitchen. From around the corner she recognized the French words for "Breakfast is served."

Barbara saw Mylok wearing a French beret. He had the breakfast all prepared as he helped her to be seated. Mylok continued with the French lesson as he recited, in French, what he had prepared for breakfast--bacon and eggs, toast, and a large glass of grape juice.

Barbara did not think twice about the grape juice. That was all she ever drank for breakfast at the university. She hated orange juice! However, it never occurred to her to ask herself how Mylok knew she did not like orange juice.

They quickly devoured their meal, for time was short. Mylok had already finished eating, so she took her toast along with her as they went to the car. It took twenty minutes to get to the university.

Along the way, Mylok decided to review with her what they had studied the night before. "Time for a 'burn in,'" he said. "That's what I call last minute review." He believed that a quick review of what had been previously studied would burn in these thoughts, ideas, and images into a person's mind.

Barbara was surprised that she remembered all she had learned the night before. Her short rest had made her feel fresh and alert. She believed that her ability to speak French had also improved due to her now relaxed state of mind.

They finally reached the university. Mylok dropped her off in front of the right building. Barbara believed that he must have gone to the university at one time himself. She recognized many of her friends already heading toward their classroom. They had arrived just in time. Barbara reached over and kissed Mylok on the cheek to thank him for his help. While she was groping for the door handle, the door opened on its own. She looked back and saw Mylok touching a button and concluded that it somehow must control the door.

As she was about to exit the car, Mylok called out, "Aren't you forgetting something?"

Barbara looked back at him in puzzlement. "What?" He handed her two ballpoint pens for the final exam. "Thanks," she said to him.

On the way to class, Barbara was greeted by a classmate. "Neat car. Is that a new boyfriend?" her friend Patty asked.

"Of course not," Barbara said while blushing. "He's just a good friend. His name is Mylok," she continued as they were about to enter the building. "We studied all night in his apartment." She knew better than to tell the truth.

Three hours later, the two buddies emerged from the classroom building. Patty casually struck up a conversation with Barbara. "It's not fair! I really studied hard this whole semester. The oral part of the exam blew me away. I think I did lousy. How do you think you did, Barb?"

"Oh, I think I passed," Barbara said, being sensitive to Patty's feelings. She knew that she had gotten at least a "B."

At the bottom of the stairs, Barbara found Mylok waiting for her by his car. It seemed to Barbara that half the university was admiring his unique vehicle. She felt like a movie star as Mylok opened the door for her as she approached.

An admirer of Barbara named, Frank, saw her get into the vehicle from across the street. Unfortunately, she didn't see Frank. This bully would often harass her. Frank and two of his friends walked toward Mylok's side of the car from across the street to look through the darkly tinted windows. As the door closed, Mylok slid his window down to greet his rival.

The tough jock looked in awe at Mylok's dashboard. Barbara just looked back at her current flame apprehensive that he might want to start something. Feeling the tension radiating from within Barbara's body, Mylok asked the body builder, "Can I help you?"

"No..." the Mr. America candidate said.

"Fine," Mylok replied, as he prevented the man from continuing with his threatening statement. Mylok quickly drove down the street, leaving the man standing with his mouth open.

Frank's buddies just laughed at him. "I'm not going to let him get away with this," Frank said furiously. Frank then hit one of his friends in the shoulder for laughing at him. "I'll kill that son-of-a-bitch," he uttered to himself as they climbed into his car. Frank's plans of asking Barbara out to lunch had just been blindsided. The angry hulk peeled out after Mylok's car in his souped up Thunderbird convertible classic.

"How do you think you did on the exam?" Mylok asked, knowing well what her answer would be.

"I think I may have aced the exam!" Barbara replied enthusiastically. "The oral part was a piece of cake. Thanks for your help. I really appreciate it. I certainly couldn't have done it without you."

"For doing so well on your final, I have decided to take you to France for lunch," he said, revealing his surprise.

Barbara laughed at what she believed to be Mylok's wonderfully dry wit. "Great. You're driving. I'll go wherever you like," Barbara said, playing along.

"We're being followed," Mylok interrupted Barbara as they came to a red light. At the last second, the T-Bird cut in front of them, nearly causing an accident. Mylok then pulled up along the left side of his rival's car.

"You idiot!" Barbara yelled at her jealous adversary through the open window. "You could have gotten us killed!" she added. Then again, she thought to herself, we probably couldn't get killed going thirty miles an hour. Frank could have dented Mylok's car, though.

"Let's see how fast this tin can is, wimp!" the hulkster said to Mylok, while trying to look past Barbara. The bully revved his engine to try to coax Mylok into a race.

Barbara turned away from the overgrown child and said to Mylok, "Let's show him what this car can do."

"This isn't a car, Barbara," Mylok said calmly. "You could call it a *plarine*. It's a *pl*ane, *car*, and subma*rine* combined into one vehicle. Believe me when I tell you that this thing really flies."

Barbara could only hear Mylok's last sentence over Frank and his friend's shouting. "Great, let's blow his doors off," she responded.

A few seconds before the light turned green, another car came around the corner from a neighboring street in front of Mylok's vehicle. The Thunderbird laid rubber as it streaked down the street. Mylok followed right behind the Thunderbird's exhaust smoke. Mylok slowly gained speed and pulled alongside of the speeding car. Barbara gave her antagonist the finger as she thought they were going to win the race. However, with an added burst of speed, the T-Bird flew away. Barbara lost all hope.

Suddenly, there were flashing lights behind them. The police were fast in pursuit. They all raced over 90 mph in the 55 zone. Play time was over for Mylok. His foot was barely a quarter down on the accelerator pedal, when he floored it. The couple left the Thunderbird virtually standing still as they shot past the gang. Barbara gasped as the G-force became intense.

"Time for that surprise I promised you for doing well on your final," Mylok said as he pulled the U-shaped steering wheel back. The windows closed air tight. Two sliding doors separated in the back of the vehicle, revealing three Apollo type rockets concealed within the trunk. However, only the three holes of the rockets showed through a vertical sheet of metal. Like the fastest of military jets, Mylok's vehicle shot straight up toward the clouds. Yet, the powerful jets were completely silent from within the vehicle.

Barbara was in shock when everything suddenly "went white" as they traveled into a cloud. She was momentarily blinded by the intense light of the cloud. Believing that they were still on the ground, she lost all thought of reality. They continued upward and went through another cloud. In a matter of seconds, the sky grew dark. The G-force eased off and Barbara's heartbeat slowly returned to normal. Looking through the windshield, all she could see were stars. "What's happening?" Barbara screamed.

"We're on our way to France," Mylok said casually. "You better put on your seat belt due to the lack of gravity up here."

"What happened to the sun?" she responded. "Where are we? I can't even see the road," Barbara said, unaware of feeling the vehicle steadily increase its speed.

"Look out the window," Mylok said with a glint of mischief in his eyes. "Don't be alarmed, but we are now skimming the earth's atmosphere. Look down," Mylok answered in amusement, anticipating her next reaction.

"Damn. We really are flying," she said after seeing the earth beneath her. "I think I'm going to be sick."

"Good," he teased about her oncoming illness. "Then you'll have room for lunch."

"I'm not kidding."

"Neither am I."

A few seconds went by. "How is this possible?" she asked in awe.

"Because you aced your final," Mylok said again jokingly. "And besides, I'm starving for a French dinner."

"Dinner? Isn't it lunch time."

"Not in France," Mylok said, reminding her of the time difference. "How do you enjoy the view of the earth?"

"I can barely see it," Barbara said, since the earth was almost directly under Mylok's vehicle.

He then rotated the space craft ninety degrees clockwise so that she could have a perfect view. Because of the lack of gravity, she did not even feel the vehicle move. She now had a breathtaking view of the earth on her right side. "Wow!" she said in disbelief. Barbara stared out the window at the clouds covering the Atlantic Ocean.

"Not too many people ever see this sight, except for possibly watching it on TV," Mylok said.

"Thank you for the surprise," she responded with tremendous enthusiasm, forgetting her fear of heights. She then leaned over and gave Mylok a kiss on the cheek. Even her fantasy man couldn't live up to Mylok.

"The surprise is just beginning," Mylok said. "You're going to love France...You'd better fasten your safety belt," he reminded her a second time. As she fastened her belt, he continued, "We're going to coast for a while, so that you can enjoy the experience of antigravity."

As the acceleration subsided, Barbara enjoyed the unusual sensation of outer space. While strapped tightly to her seat, Barbara thought of how lucky she was. She thought of all the joys in life as she watched the earth go by outside her window. Knowing that they were not the only objects in space, she thought of the neighboring satellites roaming around them. Barbara then asked Mylok rather alarmingly, "Won't we be picked up by radar?"

"Probably. You do know, it wouldn't be the first time the world's governments picked up a UFO reading," he said.

"Won't they shoot us down then?" she asked, fearing that they might be attacked by nuclear rockets or a laser satellite.

"I never really thought of that," Mylok said. After sensing Barbara's heart skip a beat, he added, "Just kidding."

"Please don't do that to me. You nearly gave me a heart attack," she said as she lightly hit him on the chest with the back of her hand.

"Ouch," Mylok said, as he grabbed his chest with his left hand. Mylok playfully pulled down on the steering wheel with his right hand as if he was in great pain. This caused the vehicle to do a couple of barrel rolls. Mylok then straightened out the wheel.

During the barrel rolls, Barbara feared for her life, thinking that they were going to crash. Her eyes were opened wide, and her fingers gripped the dashboard so tightly that her knuckles turned white. After a few seconds of regaining her exposure, Barbara looked over toward Mylok. His head was bobbing up and down and right and left, as if he was enjoying the beautiful view. The slight grimace on his face gave him away. He was still playing around! "Stop it!" she said, giving him a second hit on the chest. Barbara continued, "I didn't hit you that hard."

"Oh, lighten up," Mylok said. "I'm just having a little fun. No need to worry about us. This vehicle is so small and traveling so fast, they would not be able to get a good fix on us by radar. If it makes you feel any better, this vehicle could handle an attack," Mylok added, knowing that it could.

Mylok then rotated and turned the miniature space craft so that it was flying backwards on its same course. This was to prevent the safety straps from causing pain by digging into the stomach and shoulder for a time.

The sun first appeared overhead. Then, Barbara enjoyed seeing the clouds pass by as the sun slowly descended over the earth. Mylok increased the tinting capabilities of the window to block out the blinding rays of the sun. As the vehicle decelerated to the appropriate speed for reentry into the earth's atmosphere, Mylok again darkened the craft's windows.

Barbara thought she saw the coast of England, before the windows went black. She started to get nervous as she remembered seeing astronauts' Apollo capsules burn on reentry. She held Mylok's dry hand with her sweaty one for reassurance. Mylok was completely at ease, she noted, as she looked at him. It looked to her like he was very confident in himself. Like he had done this many times before.

Again, the flying car turned around like a plane coming in for a landing. Reentry into the earth's atmosphere was over quickly. Due to Mylok's superb technology, it felt to Barbara as if she were decelerating her car with a drag racing parachute.

Within fifteen minutes from take off, they had traveled over 3,500 miles. Barbara could now see the coast of France. She could not believe the beauty of the landscape. The valleys, fields, and rivers were all breathtaking. Never before had she seen such sights. Never before had she flown, especially in a car. In the distance, Barbara believed that she could now see the Eiffel Tower. It became more obvious as they approached.

Barbara's only concern now was how to land without being detected by anyone. Mylok didn't care. He was out to have some fun. He decided to land at a busy intersection. With the aid of his vehicle's computer, he was able to time the intersection when the streets had the walk sign on and the red lights. With all the right lanes across from the intersections free, landing would be easy. This was logical?

People looked in wonderment as a soaring silver car flew only a few feet above their heads. One man accidentally hit another car from the rear as he watched Mylok's car land. "Are you crazy?" Barbara asked in disbelief.

"Why?" he asked, as the back wheels gently hit the ground and the car continued down the street.

"They might spot us!" Barbara exclaimed in concern for their safety from the French government. She did not even have a passport to enter France.

"I'm sure they already have," Mylok replied coolly. "Not very often does one see a flying car."

"That's what I've been telling you! You're going to get us into big trouble," Barbara continued in panic.

"Who's going to tell what they saw?" Mylok asked. "Any official would think they were crazy. Besides, we were traveling too fast for anyone to get a good look at us." To ease her anxiety, he continued, "Also, they'll be out looking for a silver car. Right?"

"Right."

"So all we have to do is to change the color of the car."

"I don't think France has any Maaco stations," Barbara said, referring to a quick paint job for the car.

"What do you think of red?" Mylok asked while all the other cars behind them were still stopped at the traffic lights.

"You're not serious?"

"We can't leave the car silver."

"Then, I guess red will be fine. It's your...whatever this is," Barbara said, uncertain what to call the vehicle.

"Then red it is!"

In a quick streak of light, the vehicle changed from silver to red starting from the front. Like a chameleon, the car changed color before her eyes as she watched through the windshield. On a street with many stores, a Frenchman bumped into a woman carrying many bundles. While admiring Mylok's car passing by, the unsuspecting man was drawn off guard at the change of colors.

Barbara giggled at the comical sight. She then turned to Mylok and asked, "Can you change it to any color?"

"Yes, any color or group of colors," Mylok told her. "You can design any pattern on the computer and it can be processed in the blink of an eye." He then showed her several patterns he designed on the car's monitor TV.

"I like that design," Barbara said with envy.

"All right. We'll save that for next time."

Mylok's colorful shirt and beret no longer looked ridiculous to her. Several other Frenchmen were wearing similar clothes. Mylok blended in beautifully, while she stuck out like a sore thumb. Barbara soon felt as though she were wearing rags, when she saw the gorgeous designer dresses all the women were wearing. She also felt self-conscious about wearing the same dress for two days straight. "I look terrible," she said.

"You can't come to France without buying new clothes," Mylok said. "My treat."

"You're too kind. I can't accept it," she said with disappointment.

"I insist. What good is money if you can't spend it to make others happy?" he insisted.

They soon pulled alongside a tight parking space. Any other person would have looked for another spot. Not Mylok. With the aid of retrorockets underneath the car, he was able to hover slightly above the street, much like a hovercraft. Tiny thrusters on Mylok's side slid the floating car into the spot with only an inch to spare in front and back. Barbara was speechless. By the time she thought of something to say, Mylok had climbed out and opened her door after rolling over the hood of his vehicle.

They browsed in the store for forty minutes looking for just the right outfit for Barbara. Mylok joined her in her search. Barbara tried on many dresses and finally found the one she had to have. Mylok bought it for her. He also bought a new outfit for himself that she picked out for him. They then walked out of the store wearing their new clothes. Barbara had the sales clerks put her old clothes in a box. After placing the box in the car, along with her new bottle of perfume (the best money could buy), they continued their sightseeing.

The loving couple, walking arm and arm, were soon passing a very expensive looking beauty shop. Mylok playfully pushed Barbara toward the front door. With a smile on his face, he said, "Time for a face job."

"No!" Barbara shouted as she tried to exit through the door, not wanting Mylok to spend any more money on her. She added, "You've already spent too much on me."

"Get in there. Don't you know that I have a reputation to uphold," he said jokingly about her messy hair. Due to her general lack of funds, she had not once had a professional haircut the entire semester.

"Oh, all right," she said, not wanting to make a scene. How does Mylok keep his hair so neat all the time, she wondered? Maybe his pet cuts his hair, she mused.

Barbara was soon seated at a sink where she had her hair washed. After sitting up to have her hair dried by a male hair stylist, she looked over toward Mylok. He was seated, reading a French magazine. Probably looking at French models, she jealously thought to herself. Mylok looked up at her, smiled, and blew her a little kiss to tease her. As she walked past him to the cutting chair, Barbara just gave him a sarcastic smile for "forcing" her to come there first.

Barbara sat in the chair, feeling self-conscious. She started to panic as she saw in the mirror that six inches of hair had been cut from her head. Occasionally, she would glance at Mylok in the mirror. While sitting outstretched on a couch, Mylok just stared at her in amusement with his arms folded over his chest. Her embarrassing situation got her quickly upset with him.

So that she wouldn't get caught, Barbara watched the hair dresser closely to correctly time her next action. She gave Mylok a dirty look, and at the same time, slid her hand from under the oversized bib and dropped it toward the floor. Then, the French hair cutter was on the other side of her. With her hand, Barbara gave Mylok several pushing actions. Mylok quickly got the message and went back to reading his magazines.

Although the ordeal was embarrassing, Barbara loved her new hair style when it was all over with. Her shoulder length hair cut curled inward. Her dirty blond hair was given some blonde high lights. She quickly ran over to Mylok and gave him a big hug and kiss for his generosity. The Frenchman smiled as he then knew that she was pleased with his creation. Barbara thought that it would be much cooler for the summer vacation. Like a true native of France, Mylok spoke to Barbara's hair stylist and tipped him generously. It was the largest tip that he had ever received in his fourteen years as a hair stylist.

The time quickly flew by and it was now time for dinner. Mylok took Barbara to the finest restaurant in all of Paris. Like a true native of France, Mylok ordered a dinner fit for a king. Unbeknownst to her, Mylok ordered the most expensive bottle of wine there. At first, the waiter just gave Mylok a strange look, figuring that the young couple would never be able to afford such an expensive bottle of wine. Nonetheless, with the customer's persistence, the waiter came around, figuring it was Mylok's neck on the line and not his.

Never before had Barbara seen such elegance in food. Every piece of food was a true work of art. Such time had to be spent in its preparation before being served. Barbara truly enjoyed each wonderfully unique taste of her meal. For dessert, she had a generous portion of chocolate cake, with a very thin sheet of edible gold laid on top for decoration.

At the end of their dinner, the waiter placed the bill on a tiny plate. He expected big trouble from Mylok, as his date had gone to the women's room to freshen up. A meal like that would set the average Frenchman back financially for several weeks. To say the least, Mylok made the waiter think twice about judging a person by his looks alone.

As he waited for Barbara to return, Mylok listened in on an older couple's conversation at the next table. They were a well-to-do Japanese couple visiting France on vacation. Like Barbara, they too had trouble speaking French. So instead, the older couple spoke only their native language to each other. They admired Mylok and Barbara, believing them to be a young loving French couple. The Japanese woman greatly admired Barbara's beauty and told her husband this.

Mylok then turned around and thanked the neighboring couple in their language for their comments about Barbara. Mylok told them how Barbara and he were also visiting the country from America. He also asked the two Japanese people about the sights they had seen so far. The older couple were amazed by Mylok's fluency in Japanese, but enjoyed conversing with someone whom they could talk with fully.

After a few minutes, Barbara came back to find Mylok in the middle of telling a joke in Japanese. Then, the middle-aged couple laughed at the end of his unusual story. The couple thanked Mylok and bid him farewell as they continued with their dinner. Mylok then turned again to face Barbara, who was now seated across from him.

"You also speak fluent Chinese?" Barbara asked Mylok, while giving up on her French. The Japanese woman again took a glimpse at Barbara to admire her tight fitting silken gown and beautiful complexion. The light blue gown was low cut in the front and backless. An additional flowered shape material acted as a sort of belt.

"Yes," he replied knowing fluent Chinese as well. "FYI, they're Japanese."

"What's the difference?" she asked in a sarcastic tone, unaware of the great differences in cultures.

"That's like saying, 'What's the difference between the United States and France?'" he said to straighten her out. "They are two entirely different cultures and speak totally different languages."

They soon left the restaurant to do some more sightseeing. The setting sun was breathtaking, as they watched it from the top of the Eiffel Tower. Barbara stared at the darkening sky, as the night lights soon took over the city of love. She held Mylok tightly around the waist in a romantic grip.

Shortly thereafter, they left the tower. Mylok proudly showed her the many sights of Paris. Time flew by as they explored the large city. The two of them started to get soaked when they got caught in a heavy down pour. There was so much more to see in Paris. Due to the rain, Mylok insisted that they spend the night in the city. That way, she could explore more of Paris the next day. What kind of position was she in to say, "No" to him? Barbara felt trapped. Mylok was her way home!

"We're getting soaked," Barbara said worrying about her new dress. "I'm completely lost. Where did we park the car?"

"On the other side of town."

"Then, we'll need to find a taxi quick."

"No need," Mylok said as he pointed to the sky. From a far distance, she could see a pair of headlights coming straight toward them. Within a matter of seconds and on its own, Mylok's vehicle soon landed in front of them.

Barbara soon found herself in a honeymoon suite. Only the best for her, Mylok insisted. However, there was only one king-sized bed, like the majority of the rooms in the hotel building. Mylok told her that he would be willing to sleep on the chair. As long as he would be able to behave himself, Barbara exclaimed that there was plenty of room on the king-sized bed for both of them.

While Barbara took a quick shower before going to bed, Mylok watched a French movie while resting on the bed in his wet clothes. After a few minutes, Barbara came out wrapped with only a towel around her naked body. When she saw him dripping on the bed spread, she said, "Mylok, you're getting the bed soaking wet."

"Then, I should probably remove my wet clothes," he replied while staring into her eyes. Mylok slowly removed his soaked shirt a button at a time. Barbara felt uncomfortable at his choice of words. Though she cared for Mylok, she deeply loved Paul. She never had an attention of cheating on Paul. Also, Barbara felt as though she was kidnapped. She did not know what she was doing there. Barbara felt that she was trapped in Paris with no way home, except for Mylok. The last thing she needed was to get on Mylok's bad side. Without a passport or the finances, how could she get out of France? Mylok then reached under the bed and handed Barbara a clothes box. "Good night, Barbara," Mylok said, as he walked to the bathroom to shower.

"Oh my god," Barbara muttered to herself after Mylok closed the bathroom door. Barbara expected that there was some sort of nightgown within the box. Upon opening the box, she found a one-piece pajamas set. She laughed herself sick after seeing the pajamas with their built-in booties. Barbara hadn't worn anything like this since she was a little girl. At least, it was dry. Mylok's understanding soon led her to feel relaxed.

While the water ran from Mylok's shower, Barbara put on her new pajamas. They were a perfect fit. Barbara then crawled into the bed and pulled the covers up. She sat up to watch the television. However, the strain to understand the French movie and the long day soon led her to fall asleep.

Mylok came out of the bathroom with a towel around his waist. He approached Barbara, who was sound asleep in bed. Mylok gently kissed her on the forehead. Taking a few steps back, he turned the lights off. Mylok then sat on the floor for meditation. As he meditated, Mylok's back glowed from the cross on his alien branded back as it has for ages past. The ceiling reflected his golden shine.

Chapter 4

"**G**ood morning," Mylok said as Barbara woke up after a long night's sleep. He was already dressed and had perfectly timed breakfast so that it was brought to their door a few seconds before she woke. "Let's eat. We still have much sightseeing left."

"Good morning," she said with a smile, remembering their previous day together. After putting on her dry dress, she joined him in a romantic little brunch.

"We came close to making the headlines today," Mylok said as he translated a small article in the local newspaper about their landing outside of Paris the day before.

"See, I told you that you would get us into trouble," Barbara laughed. Out of the French article, she could only make out their arrival time and "voiture," the word for car. Barbara laughed even harder as Mylok told her about one man's story of their landing.

When they finished eating, they decided to leave the hotel room to visit the Louvre. It was probably the finest art museum in the world, she thought. Before they left, Barbara took the red rose from its small vase. It had been given to them on the breakfast table that had been wheeled in for their brunch. As a token of their stay in Paris, Barbara wished to press the rose in her scrap book at school.

Time flew by quickly at the Louvre. Barbara was in awe of the detail of the heaven and hell paintings. She loved to see the cupids and the statue of "David," even though she was slightly repulsed by the statues of the naked women. Barbara believed it was time to head back to the university. Even though Barbara was having the best time in her life, she wanted to say goodbye to her roommate for the summer. Also, the dorm room had to be cleaned out by tomorrow. Her aunt and uncle were expecting her to spend her summer vacation at home with them, before returning in the fall for her senior year. "We should leave shortly," Barbara said. "I got to get back to the dorm room to clean it out. Also, I would like to say goodbye to my friends before they take off for the summer."

"I have to make one quick stop before we leave," Mylok said.

"Where to?"

"The Egyptian section of the museum."

"Are we going to visit some ancestors?" Barbara asked jokingly.

"Something like that. It's the reason we are here."

"I thought it was because I aced my French final," she said with a sour look.

"Sorry, but this is a business trip."

They soon approached the mummy section of the Louvre. After a little sightseeing, Mylok suggested, "It would be a good idea to hit the women's room before our long trip back."

"I'll be right back," Barbara said, as she headed toward the restroom.

Mylok stood in front of a mummy, which was protected by a plexiglass case cover. He extended his right palm one inch over the top of the case covering. While exhaling, he tapped the cover and the plexiglass shattered. Eight people turned toward the sound of the breaking glass in disbelief, as Mylok tore through the cloth covering of the mummy and into his chest cavity. Mylok then pulled out of the ancient priest a glowing organic orb of mystical powers, about the size of a baseball. Due to its organic properties, this orb never showed up on scientists' X-rays. Therefore, it had been protected for five thousand years.

After transferring the energy of the orb to himself, the orb transferred to nothingness. Then, a burst of energy exploded from Mylok's chest, paralyzing the eight people in the room with him. Mylok then greeted Barbara as she walked out of the restroom. Unbeknownst to Barbara, the two of them left the museum after committing the perfect crime.

Before returning to America, she picked up many small gifts for herself and her friends. Her roomie, Roo, would never believe that she spent two days in Paris with Mylok. They soon drove down the busy street leaving Paris behind. Due to traffic hour, the street was jammed with cars.

A young Frenchman, about their age, was admiring Mylok's red, mid-sized sports car from beside him. While soaking up the rays from the hot sun, the Frenchman continued to stare at Mylok's darkly tinted window from his white convertible sports car. Barbara started to feel a little uneasy, believing that everyone was looking at the unique design of Mylok's car.

While Barbara was flipping through her postcards of Paris, Mylok decided to strike up a casual conversation with the Frenchman beside him. He slid the window down to talk to the young native. "Great day today," Mylok said in French to the driver of the neighboring car.

"Oui," the Frenchman replied. He then told Mylok of a news broadcast, which he heard a few seconds before. The Frenchman continued with his story of a broken down truck up the street. Because the truck blocked the entire street, they would be stuck there for some time until the truck could be moved out of the way.

Barbara was becoming impatient about having to wait when Mylok translated the message to her. As she continued to browse through her postcards, slightly bored with having to wait in the heavy traffic, Mylok figured it was time to have a little fun. He said to Barbara, "Time to get out of here."

"You wouldn't dare," she told him.

"Did you happen to read the morning paper?" Mylok asked the Frenchman. Mylok pointed to the computer's TV screen, which showed Barbara the translation of the Frenchman's response.

"Yes, why do you ask?" the computer screen showed Barbara in English.

"Did you happen to read that crazy article of a flying silver car?" Mylok asked his poor victim.

"That was crazy all right," the Frenchman replied. "The morning TV news said that it was a plane making a crash landing. They said the plane was recovered last night. They never did get that story straight."

"It just so happens that my girlfriend and I were there yesterday. We saw no plane," Mylok exclaimed in French.

"You must have just missed them take it away," the Frenchman said.

"The paper said that several eye witnesses said it was definitely a car," Mylok tried to convince him.

"They must have been drunk," the Frenchman responded. "Cars can't fly." Barbara slid to the floor, laughing herself sick after reading the computer caption on the car's screen.

That was all Mylok needed to hear. "I assure you that it is quite possible," Mylok said as the car changed from red to its original color of silver. The Frenchman's mouth dropped open, as he looked at the change of colors. "Farewell. Come by some time and visit us on Mars," Mylok offered with his dry sense of humor.

Barbara thought that she was going to pass out from laughing so hard. Mylok then hit the thruster rockets under his car for vertical lift. As the car lifted slightly higher than the white sports car, Mylok's back doors slid open, revealing the three main Apollo type rockets. The Frenchman looked on in awe. As he saw the silver bullet streak toward the heavens, the Frenchman believed that Mylok's car was heading for Mars.

Soon Mylok flew past the coast of France. After his practical joke, he brought the car quickly downward. He was flying a matter of inches above the surface of the Atlantic Ocean, and Barbara believed that he was flying low to avoid being detected by radar. For whatever reason, there was no space ride this time. Her laughing at the Frenchman soon stopped when the blinding sun hit her on the right side of her face.

"Shouldn't we be heading directly into the sun to go back to the university?" Barbara asked Mylok, knowing that their trip back to the university should be due west. Because the sun sets in the West, she knew that they were heading in the wrong direction. Barbara suspected that they were heading more southward, since the sun was on her right side.

"We're heading back to my place," Mylok said. "There's plenty of time tomorrow to clean out your room. I'll even give you a hand. However, it's now time to eat. You wouldn't believe the dinner I have planned for you."

"Great," she said. "The cafeteria food at school will kill you." She was sick of eating the same food for three years now. Barbara would often eat at the restaurant where she worked, but they still charged her half price on anything she ordered, which got expensive after a while. On occasions, her boyfriend, Paul, would take her out to eat. However, this was mainly on the weekends due to her work schedule.

Besides wanting to say goodbye to Roo and clean out her room, Barbara's aunt and uncle were expecting her to return home for the summer vacation. Her real parents had died in a car crash when she was three years old. Because she was so young at the time, Barbara could only remember her parents by looking at old photographs of them. She had lived with her father's sister for the past seventeen years. Barbara even legally changed her last name to her uncle's. Because her aunt had five children, Barbara often felt neglected over the years. She knew that Mylok was the best thing that had ever happened to her.

After traveling considerably faster than the speed of sound for a few minutes, Mylok announced, "Hold on tight for braking." Barbara learned on the trip over to always fasten her seat belt and shoulder strap. She had already fastened her belt when she entered the car.

"Whee!" Barbara screamed with excitement as the flying car snapped 180 degrees in the opposite direction. As the car flew backwards, Mylok again hit the switch for the rockets. The couple sank comfortably backward into their soft seats, as the car decelerated rapidly. Due to the three powerful rockets, the ocean's water was shot into the air and over the car. Like a surfer shooting the curl, the ocean quickly engulfed them due to the thrusting rockets.

After braking to a little over two hundred miles an hour, Mylok again turned the car around. He was now heading in the same direction the car had been heading before. Barbara was more than thrilled with the ride, believing that it was more fun than a roller coaster.

"Hold on for reentry," he said. Then, Mylok pulled back on the steering wheel. The car rose into the air. He did this to penetrate the ocean's surface more cleanly. Otherwise, like a flat stone skipping along a pond, entering the ocean at such a low angle might cause them to bounce off a wave, which could result in a fatal accident. Therefore, a steep entry angle was needed. After a couple of seconds, he pushed the steering wheel forward. The car plummeted toward the ocean's surface.

"Ahhhh!" Barbara screamed, convinced that she was now going to die. Like a falling rock, the car vanished into the ocean's depth, leaving behind a tremendous splash.

The impact was not all that bad, Barbara thought. The pull from her seat belt and shoulder strap was not much greater than what a parachutist would feel. "I think I'm deaf," Mylok said with a laugh, referring to Barbara's loud scream.

"Sorry," she said as the car slowed down sharply due to the steadily increasing water pressure. The submerged car was soon two miles beneath the ocean's surface and heading steadily downward. The ocean's depth quickly made everything around them pitch dark. "How do you know where you're going? You're going to kill some fish," Barbara exclaimed with concern. Mylok then turned on the car's headlights as a joke. In truth, he didn't need them due to the vehicle's built-in sonar monitor.

Barbara was shocked when she saw a hammerhead shark swim by. However, her fear left when she remembered she was in the safety of the car. The air tight vehicle was able to go farther down than most submarines. Barbara did not even note any change in air pressure. Mylok's thin windows were definitely not made of anything from the world that she knew about. How could a car withstand such extreme pressure and not be crushed like a walnut? She wondered to herself.

The car's headlights soon reflected a flat downgrade in the ocean floor. As Mylok adjusted the car from a computerized monitor, they finally reached the ocean's bottom bed. The downgrade led them to an enormous tunnel within the ocean's floor. The entrance looked much like a runway for airplanes. Why was the opening so large? She thought. Barbara then thought of all the unexplained disappearances within the Bermuda Triangle.

After they had entered the tunnel, the huge sloping downgrade lifted upward due to its hydraulic lift. This concealed any sign of a tunnel entrance. The car continued down the long landing strip. Each light within the tunnel became brighter as they continued down the runway. Barbara's heart rate quickened. She felt as though she were in a James Bond movie. Nevertheless, this was no movie; it was reality.

They soon entered a huge atmospheric chamber. Barbara heard a sliding door close behind them. The salt water was quickly pumped out of the huge empty room. Due to the possible shock that was coming, Mylok turned to Barbara and said, "Brace yourself for what you are about to see."

"What?" she asked softly as the door in front of them slowly came down, revealing the secrets of the Bermuda Triangle. She looked in wonder at a huge hangar about a square mile in size. Within this hangar, she saw hundreds of UFOs of all shapes and sizes. As they passed by, Barbara saw a few planes that she remembered from the past. She saw many planes from the first and second World Wars and several jet fighters.

As they continued to drive up and down several aisles, she saw many ships on display as if they were in a museum. They ranged from old Viking ships of ages past to more modern vessels. They also ranged in size from small sailing boats to large ocean liners. She then remembered that they had mysteriously disappeared many years ago. Barbara soon asked, "What happened to all the people?"

"A few died in battles amongst themselves," Mylok told her. "Many have died because of old age."

"How about the others?" Barbara demanded.

"They are very much alive," he said. "You will soon see. Many were returned to their home lands with great knowledge. They continue to live on the outside world. Thousands wished to stay here."

"Where are they?"

"You will soon see them."

"Aren't you afraid that people from the outside world will someday find you down here?" she asked with some concern.

"They haven't yet," Mylok exclaimed. Soon Mylok pulled over to a vacant lot, and the car's doors opened up for them. They then walked over to an open doorway. The two of them walked into a huge empty room. As they walked, Barbara thought that hundreds of people were walking toward them. After approaching closer, she realized that they had been moving toward a huge mirror. The strange mirror reflected the many images of Mylok and Barbara.

"This is weird," she said about the magical mirror.

"This is only half the fun of this unique mirror," Mylok exclaimed. He then uttered something in his native language. "You have never seen yourself as others see you." The multiple images of them were then cut down to just the two of them. However, their reflections were wrong, Barbara knew. In her place was Mylok's reflection and vice versa. Mylok then left her to do a flying leap in the huge empty room. The mirror then froze his jump in midair. Mylok no longer cast a reflection.

"That's crazy," Barbara said as she shook her head. Barbara was caught off guard when her reflection did the opposite of what it was supposed to do. She stared in awe at her reflection. Something was terribly wrong. As she slowly raised her right hand, her left hand raised in the mirror. "This is fu...," she said under her breath.

"Stop admiring yourself in the mirror," Mylok said jokingly. "Come along." Barbara then walked toward him. However, her reflection did not follow her in the Mylokian mirror. As she walked, Barbara again looked up at Mylok's frozen leap. They then continued toward the next doorway. Before Barbara could say anything to Mylok, she saw her reflection walking past her in the opposite direction. While continuing to walk, Barbara looked over her shoulder to see her reflection staring back at her as they departed from one another.

They passed through the new doorway, and into an enormous living room. This was an entirely different room from Mylok's bedroom. This was a room for an Egyptian monarch.

"Wow. Is this yours, too?"

"Yes."

"How many rooms do you happen to own, if you don't mind me asking?" Barbara asked. Also, she hadn't seen any other person so far, except Mylok's pet, Max whatever it was, not counting the dragon.

"I myself own over ten square miles of rooms," Mylok said modestly. He really had closer to eleven square miles. "Each one is unique in design, architecture, and size...I'm hungry. How about you?"

"I'm starving."

"Good," he said as he led her to a huge dressing room. Out of thousands of dresses, he picked one out for her. Barbara stared at the full length, white satin gown. The upper chest, back, and legs were covered with transparent lace. The thick heavy belt appeared to have genuine emeralds embedded in white leather. Her necklace looked like it was 24 Karat gold. As Mylok left her to dress, she thought that she was heading for a masquerade party; she was going as a pharaoh's sovereign.

After a few minutes, he asked, "Are you ready?"

"I guess so," Barbara responded. She looked at Mylok and started to laugh at the way he was dressed. He looked like an ancient Egyptian Pharaoh. His over sized gold necklace and his white and blue striped hat with a small gold cobra on the front made him look like King Tut.

"You look beautiful," Mylok said as he helped her on with the necklace.

"I haven't got a clue how to put these on?" Barbara said about the sandals with two foot strappings.

Mylok slipped the sandal onto her dainty foot and wrapped the straps three times around her leg to just below her knee. Mylok didn't tie a bow, instead, he tucked the ends into the top loop just above the calf. After repeating himself on the opposite leg, he then offered his arm to her like a gentleman. "Stay cool," Mylok said as they walked through another doorway together. Of all the rooms he might have chosen, he had to lead Barbara to the one with the dragon. How can I stay cool with that dragon staring at me? She thought.

They soon approached the entrance to the great hall. Barbara looked down the hall in shock. Mylok did say that she would see people, but this was ridiculous. Along the walls of the quarter mile hallway were hundreds of men dressed in white robes. They were guards of Mylok, she soon figured out. As they passed by, the guards saluted. When Mylok walked by, each guard would touch his heart with open hand and then extend his arm in the direction of their path. Each hand would stop at exactly waist level for every guard.

They quickly reached the altar of Mylok's departed father. He led her to it, which was now on their left side. A few feet in front of the altar, Mylok dropped his hand to his side and removed Barbara's hand from his arm. He then asked Barbara, "Please kneel with me." As if in prayer to his father, Mylok knelt down in front of the altar. She joined him by his side and lowered her head. After Mylok uttered a few words in his native language, they continued their journey down the great hall of carved memories.

Barbara looked on with amusement. Her eyes and head wandered around the hall. She felt a little self-conscious about her royal treatment. Each guard just looked straight ahead. It seemed as thought they stared at the eyes of the guards across from them on the opposite wall fifty feet away. Mylok did nothing but look straight ahead. Barbara looked at him and figured that she should do the same. It was very hard for her to keep a completely straight face, for she thought they all looked a little silly.

As they continued on, Barbara grew nervous, not knowing what to expect next. She had no idea what Mylok was up to. He was leading and she was simply following along, holding onto his arm. Barbara's nervousness soon led her to tighten her grip on Mylok's arm. He knew that such an experience had to make her a little uneasy, so he turned to Barbara and smiled at her. "Relax," he said to ease the tension. "You're doing fine. This isn't a funeral you're going to."

"I don't know what to say or do," Barbara whispered back to him, not wanting any of the guards to overhear her. Unbeknownst to her, she need not have been concerned, since none of the guards spoke a word of English.

"Don't worry about it," he again said to comfort her. "There is no need to be uptight over a little dinner." For some reason, his words didn't make Barbara feel any more relaxed. At least, her apprehension helped her to stop giggling at the way everyone was dressed.

They soon passed the doorway at the end of the great hall. Strange ancient horns were blown to announce their arrival. The enormous room was dimly lit. Along with the two Sphinx statues, only the stairs and doorway were lit by the lava ceiling. Mylok then stopped at the top of the stairs with Barbara at his side.

Barbara looked down the stairs and believed that she heard sounds from the dark floor below them. The long horns were almost deafening as they continued to blast away. She looked hard at the floor beneath them, sensing some movement. However, it was too dark to see clearly.

Mylok just stared out at the dark room like a mummy. Then, for some unknown reason, the horns stopped. Mylok soon spoke out loudly a few words in his native tongue. Barbara stared at him, trying to figure what he was talking about.

Barbara looked to the ceiling above her. The tinted dome window/ceiling became lighter, letting the reddish light again fill the room. As she started to look down at the floor, Mylok turned to look at her. "Happy birthday," he said with a smile. At the same time, thousands of people beneath them cheered Mylok's speech.

Barbara laughed out loud at Mylok's terrible timing in his attempt to be humorous. Then, she nearly died of embarrass-ment when she saw that thousands of pairs of eyes were all watching her. Nevertheless, with Mylok's people cheering him so loudly, she could not have been heard if she screamed at the top of her lungs. The cheers thundered through the great dining hall. Barbara then told Mylok, "You know that my birthday is four months away." Mylok winked at her, verifying that he already knew that.

Mylok then led Barbara down the many stairs toward an empty dinner table. She held on to Mylok's arm for dear life, hoping she would not trip over her long gown and fall down the stairs. Barbara felt like a monarch. Heaven forbid that she should make a spectacle of herself by falling down the stairs. She felt so conspicuous, she already wished that she were dead.

All the people were soon talking among themselves at different tables in tongues foreign to Barbara. When they were seated, hundreds of waiters entered the room from many doorways along the walls. The waiters paraded the food along the hundreds of long tables. It seemed that every waiter that passed them served something different. Most of the food was foreign to Barbara. Mylok aided her well in choosing things that she would like.

Two waiters soon approached the table with a large rack of meat. It looked to Barbara like half a cow. The meat was still steaming hot. Mylok gestured the waiters to serve them. A third waiter cut them each a large portion of meat. That alone was a meal in itself. Barbara noticed that if someone held his hand over his plate, the waiter would continue on to the next table. Barbara got the hang of it fairly quickly.

"Do you know anybody here?" Barbara asked Mylok while looking out at the thousands of people.

"I know every person," Mylok said.

"Oh, come on. You know every person here?"

"Yes, since their birth," Mylok said with a straight face. Barbara figured that he had to be joking. Looking at a table not far from them, Barbara estimated that each person there had to be over sixty years old.

"Then, why didn't we eat with any of them tonight?"

"Very few speak your language," Mylok exclaimed. "It would have made you feel ill at ease. I wanted you to enjoy yourself."

"I guess you're right. Thank you for being so considerate," she said with a smile and went back to eating. Barbara wanted to kiss him, but figured it was not the thing to do in front of thousands of people. Sensing that, Mylok then kissed her on the cheek just as she took another bite of her dinner. The meal seemed endless, with the vast variety of meat, seafood, bread, vegetable and fruits--much of which she had never seen before. The diversity of food seemed three times greater than anything she had every seen on the movie screen of any medieval ruler's dinner table.

"Don't feel that you have to finish your plate," Mylok said.

"Thank you. I'll burst if I eat another bite," Barbara said, blushed as an older gentleman glanced over at her while talking to another man. She asked, "Who is he?"

"That's Jack Turner," Mylok said. "He's eighty-three years old and he happens to be one of the few American born people here tonight. I'll introduce you to him after dinner." Barbara felt like she stuck her foot in her mouth on that one.

Their wine and water glasses were always kept full by attentive waitresses. After half finishing her sixth gold cup of wine, Barbara began to feel tipsy. A waitress came by to serve her more wine. Barbara held her hand over the golden goblet, indicating that she had enough. The teenage girl reacted with fright at Barbara's refusal to accept her wine. Mylok told Barbara, "Please, let her fill your cup." Barbara removed her hand and her goblet was refilled for the seventh time. Mylok then spoke to the young girl in his language to ease her fright. The wine girl smiled at Mylok, curtsied, and went on her way.

"I can't finish all of this," she exclaimed to Mylok. "Why did you have her refill my glass?"

"It is our custom," he told her. "Here, food and drink are plentiful. A full goblet is always sacrificed to the Great Powers in thanks for their kindness."

Barbara figured the "Great Powers" was Mylok's term for god. "What a charming custom," Barbara said, although she herself was an atheist. The only time that Barbara went to church was for her friend's wedding.

Barbara soon called an end to dinner. She felt like she had eaten more than she could handle. Mylok then helped her up from her chair. Remembering his promise, he walked Barbara over toward the table where Jack Turner was sitting. Being shy at meeting people for the first time, she hoped that Mylok had forgotten. What was she going to say to him?

"Jack, I would like you to meet Barbara Sampson," Mylok said to his old friend, while placing his hand on Jack's shoulder. Barbara expected to be talking to a feeble old geezer, and was surprised to find he looked about sixty. Jack was in excellent condition for a man of eighty-three and well spoken, too.

"It's been a long time since I've spoken English to a beautiful young woman," Jack said to Barbara.

"I take it you speak fluent Egyptian?" Barbara asked the old man.

"Mylokian," Jack corrected her. "You will soon see that you have a lot to learn." Mylokian? Barbara thought. Who are all these people that speak a common language created by Mylok? Jack's words shook Barbara up quite a bit. Jack continued, "I've known Mylok now for forty-nine years, since his people saved me from drowning." Barbara was speechless. It would be impossible for him to have known Mylok for forty-nine years. Mylok did not look to be a day over twenty-five. Barbara then thought that Jack must have been a feeble old man after all. He was losing his memory!

Mylok interrupted the conversation when he saw that Barbara was speechless. Mylok asked his old friend, "How is the project going, Jack?" The lively old man responded to difficulty he had on the project in the language he knew best--Mylok's language. "I'll drop by to give you a hand tomorrow," Mylok said in English so that Barbara could understand at least something.

Mylok soon left his old business buddy. As they walked away together, Barbara found she had a thousand questions to ask. "What did he mean Mylokian? How can he have known you for forty-nine years?"

"It is time that I explain everything to you," Mylok said. "Come. I will show you."

Barbara pulled on Mylok's arm to stop him from walking. "I want to know now!" she demanded.

Mylok looked at her, disappointed by her sudden outburst. He explained to her, "You will have to come with me to see and understand what I'm about to tell you, Barbara. Please, trust me."

"I'm sorry. Please forgive me. This is all too new to me," Barbara said.

"I already have," he said with a smile. "Let's go."

They left the thousands of people still enjoying their dinner and conversation. They approached a hallway cut into the stairs that they had come down when they arrived for dinner. The tunnel like exit reminded her of the ones in football stadiums.

The tunnel was dimly lit. It was much smaller than the one at the top of the stairs. This one could only fit about three people across from wall to wall. It seemed creepy to her. The decorative carvings on the walls made the tunnel-like hallway seem like the ones entering the pyramids. If they kept going in the same direction, they would soon be under his father's memorial tomb. Unless, the tomb extended farther down here. Barbara felt chills running along her spine. She had no idea where Mylok was leading her.

At the end of the hallway was a room with three doors with large panels of colors. They stood in front of one of the doors. Barbara recognized the panel of colors from before. It looked much like the one in front of Mylok's bedroom, only larger. Mylok explained, "This doorway is much like your elevators. However, it can travel up or down twelve miles at the speed of light. As well as traveling vertically, it can also travel horizontally."

"You're saying that you can travel anywhere in the world with this?" Barbara said, trying to understand.

"No, only to other doorways like itself within this world," Mylok explained. "It operates much like the telephone, as I mentioned to you before at the apartment." As Mylok continued to talk, a group of six people entered the room behind them. "Watch them," Mylok told her. The leader of the group pushed a few of the colored lights. Mylok then explained, "After you dial your location, then you enter."

"I understand now," Barbara said as she saw hundreds of floors flash before her eyes in less than a second. Then, the six people entered into a different hallway, leaving the two of them in the room alone. Before Mylok could press the colors on the panel, two women walked by in front of them down their own hallway. While admiring their futuristic outfits, Barbara peeped around the corner to see where the two women were heading.

Barbara snapped her head back, realizing what she had just done. She thought, What would have happened if Mylok had pressed the buttons with my head in the location doorway? Seeing Mylok press some colored buttons, she grabbed his arm. "You could have killed me," Barbara shouted at him. Barbara believed that her head would have been severed from her body, if the floors were to change.

"That's a logical statement," he said with a diabolical grin. "It is possible to divide one's body between two dimensional..."

"Stop it, Mylok. You're-you're crazy" she started to cry then, and began moving away from him.

"It would be impossible to get hurt," Mylok tried to explain. "I care for you," he said as he grabbed her and gave her a kiss. "You know I wouldn't let you get hurt. As I was about to tell you, the doors have safeguards to prevent injuries."

"You must think that I'm the crazy one," she sniffed through tears.

"No. You have to learn to listen to your world before making any snap decisions." He then wiped the running mascara from her cheeks with the inside of his white robe. After she smiled, he continued with his instruction. He pointed to the top of the color panel and explained, "This tells the person which location they will enter."

"That would be helpful, if I could read Egyptian...or is it Mylokish, like Paul said?" Barbara asked.

"It is known as Mylokian in the English language." He continued as they walked through the doorway, "I developed a much higher form of Egyptian hieroglyphics and language. Just look at the change of your own English language since Shakespeare's time." They emerged from the doorway into a futuristic hallway. It was a big change from the one they had just left. The change was like traveling five thousands years through time, thought Barbara.

While walking down the hall, Barbara could not get over how silly Mylok looked in his King Tut costume. She broke into a little giggle. "Why are you dressed like that?"

"I think that's fairly obvious."

Barbara thought for a few seconds, trying to figure out what he meant. After all of this time, how could she be so stupid, she thought. The hundreds of respectful guards, the horns, their grand entrance at dinner, the cheering of his royal subjects were all dead giveaways--not to mention what he was wearing. As Barbara gulped, she painfully asked, "You are their king?"

In an English accent, he answered her, "By Jove, I think she's got it."

Barbara dropped to the floor in shame for having hit royalty. Heaven help me, she thought, for the way I have treated him all this time. She literally threw him out of his own bed. While on her knees, she begged for forgiveness, "Please forgive me, your majesty. I didn't know." She started to cry again. "I don't even know what to call you," she whimpered.

"I ask of you...," he told her, as she felt that she was about to have a heart attack, "Call me by my first name." Mylok smiled while looking down at her. "Don't go changing yourself because of me. I don't expect any special treatment. Unlike your world, my leadership isn't a dictatorship, but a friendship." Mylok helped her to stand up. Again, he wiped the running mascara off her face. Then, he demanded of her jokingly, "And stop crying. You're making a mess of my sleeve." Mylok showed her the black stains on the inside of the sleeve of his white robe.

"Sorry," Barbara sniffed, while again smiling at his humor.

"Let's go."

"Where are we going?" she asked, fearing that it was not going to be a pleasant place.

"The computer room."

"Good," she said, reassured by his understanding of her situation. "I studied a couple of computer courses at school."

"You've never seen a computer like this, I'll bet," Mylok told her. Before they turned the corner, he changed the subject. "You must be getting tired of walking."

"I could use a rest," Barbara hinted as she saw some of the most unusual motorcycles she had ever seen. There were three wheelless, two seater bikes. These transporters floated above the ground on an energy field much like a hovercraft.

Mylok climbed on the right side of one of the vehicles behind the steering wheel. Barbara joined him close by his side in the passenger seat.

"Hold on tight to the bars in front of you," Mylok said. Barbara had been sitting straight up in the seat. She then crouched down like Mylok and grabbed the two diagonal bars in front of her. The back of the long black chairs hooked slightly upward around the end to prevent them from sliding off. Barbara placed her feet in two chrome stirrups that were slightly larger than her feet. The foot rests were built into the vehicle on diagonals to conform to the human anatomy.

The design of the flying craft looked much like two snow mobiles side-by-side. Barbara thought that the controls were much like a motorcycle's. Mylok hit the accelerator, and the blue machine streaked down the long hallway. Barbara held on for dear life. She had never been on a regular motorcycle, let alone one that actually flew. Barbara noticed many doorways fly past, but was unable to see inside any of them because of their high speed.

The vehicle was fairly silent, thought Barbara, for all the strain that must have been placed on the engine. All she heard was a slight "whooshing" sound from the air being sucked into air vents on both sides of the flying machine. The craft had a streamlined front with a small grill which measured about a foot across. The three intake vents in the front passed through the engine and then fed into a rocket in the rear. The rocket itself must have been about two feet in diameter, she thought.

The hallway seemed to go on for miles. With the soothing breeze blowing in her face, she soon began to relax and enjoy the ride. She shouted to Mylok, "How fast are we going?"

"Two hundred and fifteen miles per hour," Mylok yelled back to Barbara. "I usually travel faster," he added, not wanting to place too much of a strain on her frail body. She noticed a flashing light on Mylok's control board. Her apprehension grew, as she thought she saw them coming to the end of the corridor. "Hold on," Mylok screamed to her. Her knuckles had already turned white from the tightness of her grip.

The corridor made a sharp right turn. There, the floor and wall rounded smoothly together, so that the turn could be taken at high speed. Because of the rounded corner, Barbara was not aware that there was a turn approaching. She assumed that they were still moving straight ahead because of the high speed at which they were traveling. Everyone understands that you have to slow down to make a turn. Nonetheless, Mylok did not.

Due to the centrifugal force, the two flew along the wall while making the right turn. Because of the G-force, Barbara's chest pressed hard on her long padded seat. After that, she wanted to walk the rest of the way.

They then entered onto another long hallway and passed several more doors and folks in the hallways. The trip seemed endless to her. Nevertheless, she knew that they had been traveling for less than a minute. Barbara heard a small buzzer in front of Mylok. She then saw a blue speck at the far end of the brightly lit corridor which grew steadily larger. Another vehicle was coming straight at them. Barbara again thought that she was going to be killed as Mylok streaked passed the approaching vehicle on the left side, instead of the right. It was just a blur to her. Having driven three years as an American, Barbara knew that she could never get used to Mylokian driving.

Finally, Mylok eased back on the throttle and the craft coasted to a smooth stop in front of a private doorway. He drove inside the arched opening to get the vehicle out of the corridor. With a mere thought, the door opened up for them. After entering the garage/room, the door slid closed behind them. Mylok sat up, turned to Barbara, and said, "Doesn't that beat walking fourteen miles?"

Barbara just stared straight ahead in a state of semi-shock. She could not forget that hard turn and the passing blue vehicle.

As Mylok pried her hands free, he cajoled, "Come on. It wasn't that bad."

"I'm all right," Barbara said, hoping to convince him. She started to tremble uncontrollably. Mylok hopped off the floating bike to help her. Barbara tried to be courageous moreover leapt from her seat. When Barbara stood on her feet, her knees buckled. Luckily, she quickly regained her balance by grabbing onto the side of the small blue hovercraft. She bravely asked, "What's next?"

"On to the central computer room," Mylok told Barbara as he helped her to the next room. Great! She thought. So far, the corridor and the "garage" reminded her of a modern hospital. The white shiny walls looked rather sterile, unlike the fancy Egyptian rooms they had just come from. Except for Mylok's bedroom, that is. Who else could cram a whole house into one room?

They soon entered the unusual room. He was right again. Barbara had never seen such a computer room. The light in the room was rather dim, but soothing to her eyes. There was a twenty foot screen in front of them. It reminded Barbara of a small movie theater, except that there were no seats.

Beneath the screen were control panels that were totally alien to her. Many long thick tubes were arranged in a semi-circular fashion, much like the pipes of a pipe organ. The metallic tubes varied between three to four feet in height, with the smaller ones in front. The tubes also varied between four to twelve inches in diameter, each of which had its own painted Egyptian symbol on the front. On top of each cylinder was a fitting dome. The domes all shone with brilliant colors.

Mylok then stood in the center of the control center. He explained to her, "This is called the Tzorb. As I'm about to show you, it is not a computer. With this device, thousands of years of cumulative knowledge is available to me alone. With the aid of this device, I am able to speak every language known to man. I can know a person before they are born, Barbara."

"That's impossible," she explained. Barbara thought to herself, And they made him a ruler?

"Open your mind. Watch and you will know it to be true," Mylok said as he held his hand over a couple of domes. The channeling of the energy from the domes soon caused a picture to be flashed on the large screen. It was a movie of an eight year old girl taking a shower. The nude little girl was singing to herself as she washed her hair.

"You're sick!" she yelled at Mylok, who then turned to look back at her with a smile. Barbara added, "You brought me here to show me a porno film?" Suddenly, the little girl slipped on the soapy floor of the bathtub. She fell and hit her face on the side of the soap dish, knocking out a tooth. Blood rushed from her mouth and the soapy little girl started to cry.

"Do you recognize her now?" Mylok asked Barbara.

"Yes," Barbara said, both horrified and amazed. "It's me."

Chapter 5

ylok had met Barbara in the woods of Maine a few years before. She may be the only key left of saving the world. The Tzorb told Mylok where to find her and of her imminent danger. He was spotted with two of his alien friends by Barbara. Mylok had saved her life by helping her find her way back to the camp ground. His continuing concern for her safety would often lead him to ask the Tzorb her state of well being. Over the years, he grew to care for her. Barbara was a desirable woman. Mylok figured he had nothing to lose in asking out the person he had secretly known and loved over the years.

The hours flew by quickly. Mylok spent considerable time traveling back in time with Barbara, showing moving pictures from the past on the unusual screen. He showed her their first date at the restaurant. Mylok explained what had really happened that night. He told her the true reason behind the mass destruction at the restaurant. It was a message that Barbara was the key to finding her grandfather's artifact. Mylok told her that he had known before hand the floor on which she had parked her car. He had known about the hoodlums before they had entered the garage. Though the Tzorb, Mylok had known all of these things.

"Oh, shoot," Barbara said.

"What's the trouble?" Mylok asked.

"I forgot to call my parents," she told him, referring to her aunt and uncle. "I was supposed to be going back home today. They must be worrying about me."

"Why don't you just call them and tell them you're going to be a day late?" Mylok asked.

"It's very late," she said knowingly. "They're probably asleep by now."

"They are still awake."

"How do you know?"

"They are watching The Tonight Show," Mylok said as he channeled his energy through the Tzorb. Barbara's aunt and uncle appeared upon the special screen. They were watching TV in bed.

"That's them," Barbara exclaimed as the telephone on the night table beside their bed began to ring.

Barbara's aunt muted the sound of the TV set with a remote control device she was holding and picked up the phone. "Hello," Mrs. Sampson said.

Mylok nudged Barbara. "Hello, Mom," Barbara said in disbelief, looking at her aunt's face on a special screen. Mylok zoomed the Tzorb around and inward like a TV camera.

"What's the matter, Barbara?" Mrs. Sampson asked, unwittingly looking straight at Barbara. However, her aunt was staring at the TV set.

"Are you all right?"

"Yes, I'm fine," Barbara said, still amazed she was calling her aunt from more than a thousand miles away from within the Bermuda Triangle. "I just called to say...I'll be coming home tomorrow."

"I understand," Mrs. Sampson told her niece, believing that Barbara wished to party an extra night at the university with her friends. "Have fun, dear. Say hello to Roo for me."

"I will," Barbara said. "See you tomorrow. Bye bye."

"Have a good night," Mrs. Sampson said, not wishing to keep her any longer. "Bye bye."

"Bye." Barbara then heard a click. Mylok had disconnected the telephone connection. Then, Barbara watched her aunt hang up. "That was incredible. How did you do that?" Barbara asked Mylok. He simply smiled back at her.

After that, Barbara enjoyed reliving parts of her past life. Mylok showed her many things she had long ago forgotten. She squirmed when she relived some of the most embarrassing moments of her life. She cried with joy when she saw the good memories of her real parents. Mylok was, of course, careful not to show her their tragic death.

Barbara soon came to believe that the Tzorb was not, as Mylok had said, just a computer. A computer could not possibly show movies of past events that had never been filmed first. If that were not incredible enough, Barbara was able to run some pictures of her current boyfriend. Barbara stopped on a particular moment of Paul's past life and froze it. Like watching a hologram, she was able to rotate three hundred and sixty degrees around Paul's picture, but with extreme clarity. No computer on earth had such control and power as this.

Mylok then took over to have a little fun. He showed her a magnified picture of a living bacteria. Barbara winced at the ugly microscopic creature. Mylok slowly zoomed out on the picture and Barbara soon realized that the bacteria was living on her eyelash right that very moment. Mylok explained that millions of bacteria live on the human body all the time.

Barbara quickly realized the power of the Tzorb. It wasn't a computer. It was like a living entity--the earth itself. Mylok's technology was years beyond anything she had ever seen or dreamed. "I'm sorry, Mylok," Barbara cried. "I never really believed you about my grandfather until I've seen this. Were you serious when you said the earth was at great risk or was that just a figure of speech?"

"It was no figure of speech."

"Oh, my god. What did he take to cause this destruction?"

"Your grandfather took our third orb of Power," Mylok explained. "To my people, it is known as the Orb of Sun-God Ra."

"From what I seen, why can't the Tzorb find it?"

"This orb is not of this world," Mylok explained. "It is a source of alien power. The Tzorb can only see matter and not manifestations of pure energy. Also, without telling the Tzorb the prosiest location to look, it is like finding a needle in a haystack. However, this haystack is the entire planet."

"You said that they're three orbs?"

"Actually, they're four in significance of the trinity."

"The holy trinity has only three: the father, son and holy spirit."

"Yet, unknown to your people, the three main pyramids house great powers, in significance of the trinity: father, son, and holy spirit, or mind, body, and chi--life force. This was the reason of our visit to the Louvre museum in Paris."

"And I thought that it was because I aced my French final," Barbara replied a little upset.

"Sorry. This was a business trip," Mylok stated. "I had to take back an article from the Louvre."

"What do you mean take back?" she asked. "Do you mean steal?" Barbara gulped.

"Yes."

"Are you nuts?" Barbara yelled. "Why would you do such a thing?"

"Our second orb, the Orb of Body [or mummification] was buried and protected within an ancient Egyptian priest," Mylok said. "This orb has powers beyond human comprehension and would be lethal in the wrong hands. The orb needed to be returned to its rightful owners for a future Mylokian project."

"What does the orb look like?" Barbara asked.

Upon the Tzorb screen, Mylok showed the Orb of Mummification. "Again, this is only a drawing. Because they're pure energy, the trinity of the four orbs cannot be seen by the Tzorb," Mylok said showing a drawing of a baseball-sized glowing object.

"How can you have a trinity of four orbs? Tri means three."

"However, like the base of a pyramid, so too, does a cross have four points," Mylok stated, while flashing an aerial view of the earth on the Tzorb's screen. "In your language, the four orbs are named: Orb of Mind, Orb of Body, Orb of Holy, and Orb of Spirit. The first orb still lies within the Aztec pyramid of central Mexico. The second orb taken from the great pyramid of Egypt was the one we obtained at the Louvre..."

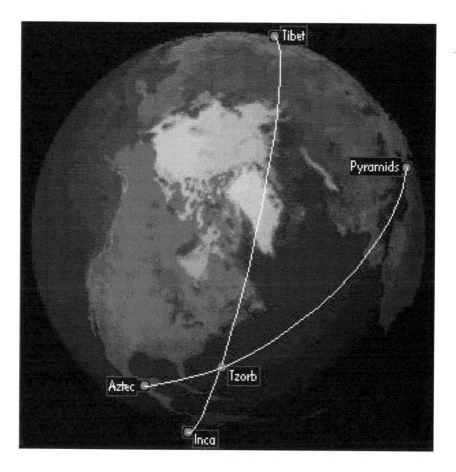

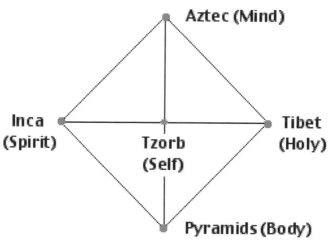

"You obtained," Barbara said, correcting him. "I had nothing to do with it."

"The third orb was taken by your grandfather and as yet has not been found," Mylok continued. "And the fourth orb is still at rest with the Inca mountain monks of Peru."

"How did the orbs get their names?"

With a mere thought, Mylok placed a diagram of the earth upon the Tzorb's screen. "The Aztec, Orb of Mind, was named for the sun always setting toward the west...for wisdom is held in light. Within Central Mexico, it was the unsettled mind that led the Aztec to defeat by Spanish conquest," Mylok said. "Egyptian mummification signifies the Orb of Body. On the left is the Tibetan Orb of Holy..."

"Your diagram has it on the right."

"But, looking upward from the Tzorb toward the stars, it would be on the left."

"OK, I'm with you."

"The left side of one's body houses the fire of the heart--the light of holiness. The right side is the creative side, the house of the spirit."

"That's probably why most people tend to be right handed," Barbara added.

"However, both left and right [holy and spirit], are a unity of yin and yang within one circle. Both are separate and opposite, but together as one self. In decapitation, the head can also be separated from the body."

"Gross," Barbara said about the thought of a beheading. "How can four separate points be united then?"

"Through intelligence," Mylok responded. "The square has the strongest of bases. These four separate points form only one intersecting origin, like the tip of a pyramid. Within a person, this center point is the inner intelligence, the 'I am,' the true self--the Tzorb."

"Then the Tzorb is at the exact center of the cross."

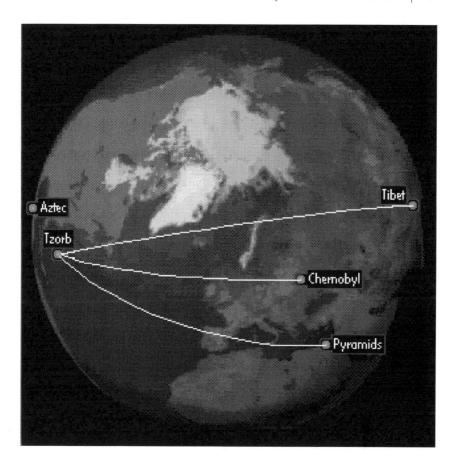

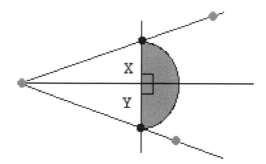

Mile Distance of X = Y

"Yes, the separating of the American continents from Africa cause a great amount of thermal energy." Mylok continued, "The world's greatest energy lives at these four points and are therefore the homes of the four orbs. The orbs then transfer this energy back to the Tzorb."

"This is incredible," Barbara mused. "What does my grandfather have to do with the Chernobyl damaged reactor leading to the nuclear fallout?"

Upon the Tzorb's screen, Mylok moved his hand over a dome erasing the cross diagram. Mylok then moved his hand to another dome. While moving his hand slightly to the right, Mylok rotated the earth eastward. She now looked downward on Europe. "When the Orb of Holy and the Orb of Body were taken from their place of rest in Tibet and Egypt..." Red dots appeared on the right side of the globe followed by the words "Tibet" and "Pyramids." "The energy drain of the Tzorb became too great," Mylok said with a red dot appearing now on the left side of the globe. The dot was soon followed by the word, "Tzorb."

"How does the Chernobyl disaster fit in?" In answer to her question, Mylok added Chernobyl to his diagram. "Chernobyl is no way near the two orbs," Barbara replied. "How does it fit in?"

With a wave of his hand, Mylok connected the two orbs and Chernobyl to the Tzorb with three white lines. She noted that the dot for Chernobyl was closer to the Tzorb than the other two orb origins. "The lack of energy from the second and third orbs led to a power drain on the Tzorb. The Tzorb was forced to bisected the difference in search for a new energy source. This new source of energy became the nuclear reactor of Chernobyl. The radioactive leakage was not due to incompetence. It was a result from the earth tearing at the reactor's core."

Barbara again explained that she had nothing more to offer about her grandfather. The fate of the earth would soon approach. Nature soon caught up with her. The long day made her very tired. Mylok led her into an adjoining room. After two hours of restlessness, she finally fell asleep on a bed Mylok had brought in specially for her. He kissed her good night and left her to enjoy her rest. Mylok returned to his control room to get down to his late night business. He removed his binding clothes and neatly placed them on hooks along the wall. Mylok then sat naked on an engraved upside-down isosceles triangle in the center of the control room. Both of his knees became two points of the triangle with his naked buttocks forming the third.

While sitting in the lotus position, Mylok looked up at the huge screen. His body formed the shape of a pyramid, the ancient symbol for seeking knowledge. He was positioned twelve feet from where Barbara and he had stood before. Mylok clasped his hands in front of his chest in prayer. As he exhaled, he channeled his internal energy toward the special screen. As he chanted in his Mylokian language, Mylok was hit in the chest with many beams of light. In quick bursts, each controlling dome struck Mylok's chest with lightning, then suddenly stopped. Still, Mylok continued his chanting. His spiritual aura soon created a golden glow around his earthly body. The golden cross again glowed on his back as it has from ages past.

Mylok's eternal life force became more intense. His internal power radiated outward in all directions, giving off a golden glow. This radiating energy caused his earthly body to levitate in mid air. He was lifted fifteen inches. With his legs still crossed in front of him, his body floated over the triangle engraved on the floor.

Soon, Mylok's thoughts were able to travel past several solar systems to his alien friend. His bald friend with twelve fingers soon appeared in front of him on the huge screen. Even though they were light years apart, they were able to communicate with each other with the galactic force around them.

The being with the oversized cranial head spoke to Mylok in thought. Neither one had to speak a word. Speaking was a waste of time. True understanding of another person can only be accomplished through the merging of both minds. The two minds must become one!

Mylok placed his hands palm up on his knees, with his middle finger and thumb touching. With his legs locked like a giant pretzel, Mylok revealed the true wisdom of a Chinese Shaolin master in meditation. This transcendental meditation was the way Mylok rested. Sleeping was also a waste of valuable time. By emptying the mind completely of all thought, a person can achieve an equivalent amount of rest with a short period of meditation as he can with a normal eight hour sleep. Dreaming clutters the mind, resulting in a restless sleep. This restlessness puts a strain on the body. Because of this, modern man requires eight hours of sleep, whereas

Mylok could achieve the same result in less than twenty minutes through meditation.

Mylok was a true master of the ancient fighting arts. His alien friends showed him how to master his body in harmony with the universe around him. By truly knowing one's body, one can learn another man's weaknesses. That person can also learn to increase his strength in specific parts of the body through energy channeling. The Chinese know of this energy as "chi" (the constantly flowing internal energy within every person). If required for self defense, this knowledge can make a person's entire body a lethal weapon. However, a wise man learns how to fight to protect the most valuable asset he owns--himself.

Soon it was morning. Barbara awoke after a good night's sleep. Today was the day she had to clean out her room in the dorm and say goodbye to Roo for the summer. Also, it was the day to head home to spend the summer with her aunt Rose and uncle Cal, moreover share her bedroom with her two younger cousins. Barbara did not care too much for that, knowing she would have to give up much of her personal freedom. Nevertheless, it was time to find Mylok and head back toward the university.

Barbara entered the room that they had been in the night before. She saw Mylok seated naked, as he continued to meditate in conjunction of communicating with his alien friends. For the first time, Barbara saw the branding on his back. She was surprised that she had not noticed it before--especially that night they had spent together in France. She thought she would have a little fun by sneaking up on him.

Coming out of his meditation, Mylok slowly lifted his head as he resumed his normal breathing. His low rate of metabolism made him very aware of his surroundings. Because of his many years of meditation, all of Mylok's senses were greatly heightened. "Good morning, Barbara," he said, before she was able to take three steps.

"How did you hear me?" she asked. "I didn't make a sound."

"I could hear your heartbeat thundering throughout the room," Mylok exclaimed as he stretched his arms out to the sides. "Before you can open your mind, you must first open up your senses."

"You must have heard me getting out of bed," she exclaimed.

"I can feel your presence," he said, sensing the heat radiating from her body. "Please do me a favor and extend your right hand out to the side." She figured it must be some special exercise as she reached out with her right arm. He then asked, "Now back five inches." Barbara moved her arm back.

"Why am I doing this?"

"Your hand is now two inches away from my robe. Do you mind handing it to me?" he asked, stretching out his right leg. Barbara looked over to her right in amazement. He was right on target. Without looking, he was able to tell Barbara exactly where she was. Barbara grabbed the robe. Barbara figured she would give it to him all right! After rolling the robe into a ball, she threw it at the back of his head.

Just before it was going to hit him, Mylok laid back and let the robe fly by. He then quickly executed three back rolls and stood up directly in front of her with his back to her. With his eyes still closed, he turned around to face her. While Mylok bent his knees, Barbara could not believe that they could be face to face. "Good morning, Barbara," Mylok said a second time, his eyes still closed, as he kissed her smack on the lips.

"Good morning," she replied as she threw her arms around him and returned his kiss. As he walked away to retrieve his robe, she asked, "Do you always sit on the floor naked?"

"Only when I meditate."

"Are you serious?"

"I'm not joking," he told her as he slipped on the robe. "I always meditate in place of sleeping. Remember that you were able to go a whole day on a half hour of rest before your exam. Besides, the cross upon my back burns my clothes."

"How is it possible for a tattoo to burn clothes?"

"When it is not a tattoo," Mylok explained. "It's a very thin sheet of metal the aliens branded to my back."

"Why did the aliens do that to you?"

"The metal acts like a receiving antenna," he said, as he walked over to get his pants. "It ties me in with the Tzorb, giving me access to its complete knowledge--but only if I seek it."

"Then the branding gives you your powers of perception," Barbara said.

"No, every person already possesses these capabilities and powers. They simply must learn to use them," Mylok responded as he slipped on his pants.

"Can the computer ever control your actions?"

"No, it is only a machine," Mylok said. "It may offer suggestions, if I choose to let it. However, it does not exercise any control over my free will...How was your sleep?"

"Good," Barbara replied. "I had a strange dream last night. I can never figure out why I have some of the dreams I do."

"You have a sixth sense," Mylok said.

"I do?"

"When you sleep, your mind is more relaxed than most people's," Mylok explained. "Dreams come from the thoughts of your past as well as the thoughts of others."

"The thoughts of others?" Barbara asked with a puzzled look.

"Yes," Mylok said. "As you know, the mind gives off certain signals."

"You're talking about brain waves," Barbara said knowingly.

"Correct," Mylok replied. "Like the waves of sound and water, the mind gives off brain wave signals. If your mind is as relaxed as a placid pool, another person can send a clear picture like that of a stone causing a ripple in a pond. Like the light from stars, brain waves, too, can travel an infinite distance."

"Then people could dream the thoughts of others," Barbara said.

"Possibly, other worlds," Mylok added.

"You mean I could dream of the same thought an alien being may have from a different world?" Barbara asked.

"Your dream and another person's thought may not always be the same," Mylok told her.

"Why not?"

"Everybody is different," Mylok explained. "Your brain will interpret things differently from other people. Take, for example, your childhood story Cinderella. If we were both to tell the same story, the wording would be different as well as the images our minds create."

"I guess you're right," Barbara replied. "That would also explain why I sometimes dream of a person that I have never met in life."

"It may have been possible for you to see that person in his real life," Mylok stated.

"Isn't that a form of telepathy?"

"Yes."

"Why is it that I'm telepathic when I sleep and not when I'm awake?" Barbara asked.

"Because your mind is cluttered due to your complex world," Mylok said. "Like the waves from an ocean's storm, your mind receives too many brain waves to focus your thought on one person at a time. When a person sleeps and the body rests, a person is free to travel to other worlds and dimensions far beyond the dream world."

"You make it sound like my soul leaves my body every night," Barbara said. "Why is it I can sleep for eight hours and not even remember a dream?"

"When you lose your sense of time during sleep, it is probably due to your eternal essence traveling to another time, world, or even dimension," Mylok explained. "Unfortunately, your brain pattern drops to the Delta or Zeta region from its normal awakening pattern of Alpha or Beta, and you forget where your soul has been."

"I'm afraid you lost me," Barbara said.

"While you sleep, you are also letting your mind rest," Mylok said. "Therefore, you forget where your soul has traveled through the night. With a little retraining of your body and mind, it is possible for you to let your body rest as you keep your mind fully conscious. Many people around the world already know this. The monks of the orient and the Hindu practitioners of India do this daily. The Americans believe them to be sleeping or resting. They couldn't be farther from the truth. These people are literally having the times of their lives in other times and dimensions," Mylok stated. "Barbara, this whole universe is here for you and is at your disposal. The power of the mind is infinite!"

"It sounds like fun. You'll have to teach me some time."

"In time, you'll be having a field day while out of body...Are you hungry?" Mylok asked. "We can go back to my room to get something to eat."

"We have to walk all the way there?" she asked, not wishing to walk a quarter of a mile down the great hall or pass through the room with that smelly old dragon. "Why don't you have one of your servants bring us breakfast?"

"No need to impose on them. It is only twenty-three steps to my bedroom, seventeen to the hovercraft and six to the teleporting doorway to get us there."

Barbara remembered her trip on that vehicle the night before. She then complained, "We have to drive back?"

"Yup!"

"Why don't you have one of those special elevators here?"

"This is a restricted area," Mylok explained. "It is off limits to all except a few maintenance workers and myself. The doorways also interfere with the operations of the Tzorb," he added as they walked to the hovercraft.

"Aren't you forgetting your shoes?" Barbara asked, trying to count each one of her steps to herself.

"No, why do I need them?" Mylok asked.

Barbara was speechless at first. "Seventeen," she counted aloud to herself. He was right again. She told him, "You should be setting a good example for your people. What type of ruler wears no shoes? What would they think?" She then climbed on board the hovercraft, as the garage door opened automatically.

"Shoes are only for appearance and to protect one's feet from rough terrain and the elements," Mylok stated, fighting for his personal dress code.

"You may catch a cold from the cold floors," Barbara said.

"The floors are warm," Mylok stated. She remembered from her first night there that was so. Mylok continued, "It's not healthy for feet to spend too much time in stuffy shoes. Besides, I haven't been sick a day since I came here."

Barbara knew it was a losing battle to try to make him wear his shoes, so she changed the subject. As they approached the doorway, she asked him about a concern she had about their safety. "What's keeping us from getting pulverized when we drive into the hall?"

"This flashes and you can hear a buzzer when another hovercraft approaches," Mylok said as he pointed to a small light on the instrument panel. If it didn't work, she thought that she wouldn't have to worry about it anyway, since they would all be dead. Mylok went on to answer her next predictable question, "The hovercrafts also have wall sensing devices to prevent them from crashing into the walls. Also, they can sense other hovercrafts and automatically pass them on the left. They virtually drive themselves."

After Mylok had explained the various safety devices, Barbara felt more at ease. The ride back was not as bad. She was even beginning to enjoy it--even though they got the vehicle up to 315 mph.

At the end of the ride, Barbara jumped off the hovercraft. Mylok turned off the engine, and she was surprised to see that the vehicle remained up in the air. She thought it must be due to an energy field like the one on Mylok's bed.

She remembered trying to poke a hole in the energy field on his bed. The field pushed back like a rubber ball. Barbara thought it would be fun to have her foot bounce back to her. It would probably be like kicking a tire on her car.

Barbara swung her leg back and kicked at the energy field under the floating vehicle. Mylok was startled when he heard a loud "bang." "Ahhh," Barbara yelled after smashing her shin on the side of the hovercraft. She hopped up and down on one leg while holding the other.

Mylok rushed to her side to aid her. "The ride couldn't have been that bad," Mylok said after he realized that she had kicked the side of the vehicle.

"I figured the field holding up this car would act like the one on your bed," Barbara explained as the reason for her misguided action.

"It should be obvious now that this is not the same kind of energy field," he said, imagining the pain she must be feeling. While offering himself as a crutch, Mylok continued, "This type of field acts more like the cushion of air on a hovercraft. The field goes around objects in its path so that it won't crush anything. This makes for a smoother ride and prevents anyone who gets run over from getting hurt. Unless, of course, you decide to kick the side."

"That's fairly obvious now," she said, her leg throbbing with pain. Mylok escorted her to the transporter doorway, as Barbara hopped there on one foot. Barbara soon realized, "I now know you aren't always right."

Mylok smiled back at her while punching in the code on the doorway's panel control. He asked her, "About what subject are you referring?"

"About how many steps it took to get to this doorway," Barbara said, grinning at him. "You told me it would take twenty-three steps to get here. It took me seventeen steps and sixteen hops to get here."

"I'm only human," he replied. Not even he could predict the entire future. How was he to know that she was going to kick the vehicle on an impulse?

His bedroom appeared before their eyes. Something seemed a little strange to Barbara. She knew that his room was down the hall from the dragon. What had happened to the hallway which was supposed to be outside his bedroom? She asked, "How many doorways does your room have, anyway?"

"Any room or hallway can have many entrances, but only one exit at a time," he told her, realizing where she was headed. He continued, "It is much like a telephone switchboard within a company. The operator, much like this doorway, may have many callers on hold. However, the operator can only talk to one person at a time."

"I see," Barbara said, lying through her teeth. She didn't know what in the heck he was talking about. All she knew was that it was possible since she had seen it with her own eyes. "What prevents others from entering here?" Barbara asked out of concern for her privacy.

"The color control panels can read the finger and hand prints of every person," Mylok stated. "This acts like a security system--a key, so to speak." Mylok sat her behind a kitchenette, which was close to the computer she used to study for French. That would have made it convenient for getting late night "munches" while studying on the computer, she thought. However, it was probably wise of Mylok not to have gotten her anything to eat, since it would have interfered with her studies. She owed Mylok a lot for having faith in her. "Thanks again for helping me pass my French final," she said.

"You're quite welcome," Mylok said as he knelt down in front of her.

Barbara remembered how easy it had been to get an "A" on her final exam. It seemed to her that they had studied only the things that were on the French final and nothing more. She then recalled the power of the Tzorb. "You knew what was going to be on that exam," she said. "Didn't you?"

"Yes," he replied. "If we were to study everything you were supposed to, you would have failed."

"Oh, you are sneaky," she responded. "I guess I'm indebted to you. At least I won't have to retake the course." Mylok then touched her aching shin. "Ouch!" she yelped.

"The bone is chipped," Mylok explained. While using his spiritual powers, Mylok healed her leg. "How does that feel?"

"The pain is all gone," Barbara said. "You're a healer too?" Mylok nodded, confirming that it was so. It was one of the many gifts taught to him by his alien friends. "How is that possible?" she asked.

"Mind over matter," Mylok responded. "With proper training, the mind can focus energy to do any will."

"I've seen spiritual healers on TV, but I never believed it until now," she said in awe.

"Hungry?" he asked.

"Starving."

The futuristic design of the kitchenette prevented her from knowing that it had been there before. Mylok pushed several buttons of light to prepare their breakfast on the meal computer. Seconds later their breakfasts emerged. She stared at the unrecognizable food on her plate. At least it smelled better than it looked, she thought. No wonder Mylok got himself something completely different to eat.

At first, Barbara just poked at the food on her plate with her knife and fork. She figured that she could make it through without eating until lunch time at the university. Mylok then placed a glass in front of her. The liquid inside the glass looked to Barbara like the scum a person would scrape off the bottom of a toilet bowl. It also had the aroma to match. The juice was thick and light brown in color. Barbara thought she was going to be sick just from looking at it, especially after Mylok went back for seconds.

The food was unique in taste and appearance just as the food the night before had been. It had a pleasant taste to it, but she still intended not to touch that juice. She nearly finished her plate and became curious about what Mylok was eating. It was not like him not to offer to share his food with her, she thought to herself. She was still hungry. After Mylok took a bite, Barbara stabbed a piece of his food to sample it.

"I wouldn't if I were you," Mylok warned, talking with his mouth full. Barbara figured that if it were good enough for him, it was good enough for her. She popped it in her mouth. It was good and juicy. It had a great meaty taste. Barbara smiled at Mylok, indicating how much she enjoyed the sample. As she started for a second fork full, Mylok grinned at her knowingly and shook his head. Barbara nodded her head as she swallowed the first bite.

The hot spicy food soon began to burn the inside of Barbara's mouth. She opened her mouth wide and started fanning it with her hand. Without thinking, she grabbed the glass and downed all the juice to quench the fire. Barbara was surprised that the juice had a good taste. After licking her lips, she exclaimed to him, "The juice is rather good, but what is that hot food you are eating?"

"Believe me, you wouldn't want to know," Mylok told her. "I warned you about how spicy it was. Maybe next time you'll listen to me."

"I've learned my lesson," she responded. For the first time Barbara looked closely at Mylok's bowl. The food in his bowl was moving. His food was still alive! A noodle had just crawled out of his bowl. Mylok stabbed it with his fork and popped it into his mouth. Barbara looked at her fork and saw tiny wiggling legs. I'm going to be sick, she thought. Barbara believed Mylok to be eating pasta Ziti. In fact, she had just swallowed a plump caterpillar.

"Good, huh," Mylok said, winking at her. Barbara nodded her head several times, fighting the urge to upchuck. That was it for breakfast for her.

Chapter 6

They flew back to the university in his silver flying car. Mylok was careful to land in a secluded area to avoid being detected. Anything to please Barbara. They then had to travel several blocks to reach her dorm room. The place looked dead.

The majority of the students had already left for the summer. A few girls still remained around the dorm building looking for the next party. Mylok had parked not far from the front door to make packing her things easier.

They went up three flights and down a hallway to get to her room. A stereo was cranked up full blast at the end of the hall. It had to be her roommate, Roo. Roo had to be the rowdiest girl on the floor--and she had the grades to prove it. Roo had been placed on probation last semester for her poor grades.

With her arms loaded with gifts, Barbara passed several empty rooms with Mylok following right behind her. It was a rule to leave the door open after vacating the building for the summer. She quickly recognized a couple of girls on her floor. Barbara never spent any time with them, so she merely gave them a casual "hello" as they walked by.

The two nameless girls watched the well dressed couple walk down the corridor. Barbara was wearing her brand new designer French dress, and she had Mylok dress to impress, too, so that she could introduce him to her friends.

Barbara soon recognized a figure emerging from her dorm room. It was Fred, one of Roo's boyfriends. Fred was all loaded down with Roo's school books, and Roo was pushing him out of the room with one hand while holding a drink in the other. Barbara and Mylok then entered her room. Roo was giving a small party for a few of her friends. The three girls were getting semi-trashed on Mountain Dew mixed with champagne.

Roo was storing some of her belongings in the dorm's attic. The university allowed most of the out-of-state girls to store some of their belongings in boxes in the attic for the summer. This saved Roo the expense of having to fly her belongings to Illinois and back just for the summer break. After filling some boxes and writing her name on them, Roo would then give them to Fred to haul up to the attic. Fred enjoyed that more than hanging around listening to the gossip of three drunk girls.

"Barbie!" the three smashed friends cried out when they saw Barbara. They were Barbara's best friends. The four of them always partied and ate together.

"This is my close friend, Mylok," Barbara announced to her friends. "We just got back from Paris. I have gifts for all of you...."

The four girls talked of the sights Barbara had seen in Paris, as they opened their presents. Barbara showed them the French postcards and told them that she wrote to all of them while in Paris. Barbara had mailed the postcards to their homes, so they should receive them when they got there. She told them everything about their trip, except for the things she knew would get her into trouble with Mylok.

"How was your flight?" Patty asked Barbara.

"It was one flight I'll never forget, being the first time I ever flown," Barbara told the girls, believing that she did not have to outright lie to them. Barbara saw Mylok smile at her for her clever response. Mylok insisted on loading the car so that she would have time to chat and finish packing.

Barbara was burning up inside because she was unable to tell her friends everything about Mylok. Barbara could not break her promise to him. They wouldn't have believed her anyway, she thought. She hardly believed it herself.

Mylok was the life of the party after he removed all of Barbara's belongings from the room. Mylok always had a clever and funny response to the girls' comments and gossip. They soon fell in love with him, just as Barbara had upon first meeting him. On several occasions, Patty commented to Barbara secretly on how lucky she was to have Mylok. Barbara was a little disappointed in Patty, because she knew fare well about Barbara's relation with Paul. Barbara explained that Mylok was just a good friend. The girls then teased Barbara, telling her that she should be playing the field.

Gradually, the room was stripped clean and the only things remaining were the beds, desks, and chairs. Fred was getting impatient with Roo to catch her flight back to Chicago. It was getting late, and Fred wanted to avoid the rush hour traffic. The three girls cried as Roo departed because she would not return until next September.

After Roo left, it was time to end the party. Barbara still had a long ride home herself. Patty had already moved back home four days ago and had come back to the university just to say farewell to Roo and Barbara.

The third girl, Debra, was a shy, homely girl. Debra had a longer ride home than Barbara did. Like Patty, she also had moved back home a few days ago and had come back to visit her only friends. Barbara often felt sorry for poor Debra. Debra never had a true boyfriend due to her weight problem. Even after she dropped Patty off at her home, it was still going to be a long trip back home for Debra.

Now, it was getting close to dinner and Barbara had already phoned home to say that she was on her way. She did not wish to impose on Mylok much longer. He was a much better sport than Fred proved to be.

After slobbering over each other for several minutes, Barbara had to depart from her close friends. They cried as they kissed and hugged each other goodbye. Barbara thought she might not ever see them again because of the great distances between them. Patty and Debra were now college graduates and thus would not be returning next semester.

Mylok started to walk Barbara out. When they reached the bottom of the stairs, Barbara looked in awe at the gift Mylok had left in front for her.

It was Barbara's car. Mylok had somehow replaced the car's windows as well as the slashed tires. As Barbara approached her car, she knew that the dents were removed and that it had been repainted. The scratches and spray painted graffiti had vanished. "Thank you so much!" Barbara said as she kissed him. "How could you do it so fast?"

"I can tell you only under one condition," Mylok told her.

"What?"

"You forget everything you have here and move in with me forever." Barbara thought he was proposing to her. He then added a major commitment on her part, "You must also understand that you can never again visit your family or friends."

"Are you asking me to marry you?" she asked, trying to understand his meaning.

"You don't understand. I can't ever marry you, no matter how much I care for you," Mylok said sadly.

"I don't understand," Barbara said. "You want me to live with you in the Bermuda Triangle, but you don't want to marry me?"

"It is not that I don't want to marry you. I would if I could. It is that I'm unable to ever marry due to my position."

"I see. It's your leadership that prevents you from ever getting married," Barbara said.

"That is correct."

"Then, what are you trying to tell me?"

"What I'm offering you is the opportunity to spend the rest of your life in my world," Mylok told her. "You'll be making many new friends. I'll be able to show you a world you couldn't ever imagine."

"You're asking me to give up everything I have?"

"Yes, we'll have to leave now."

"I can't even say goodbye to my family and friends?"

"No. What could you tell them?"

"That I'm living with you."

"Where can you say we're living?" Mylok said. Barbara realized he had a point. "No one must know of me. My world depends on that. You know that."

"They'll worry about me."

"It is the only possible way," Mylok said. "Secrecy is of the utmost importance. Your life may depend on that. People mysteriously disappear ever day."

"I have plans for my future after I graduate."

"That future couldn't compare to the future you'll have with my people," Mylok stated. "Life is short, Barbara. There is no sense living it in a struggle, if you don't have to."

"What if I don't like living in your world?"

"You have the option to return home here anytime you wish," Mylok said. "However if you do, it wouldn't be likely that we would ever be allowed to met again for the possible harm it could cause to my world. You're already a great enough of a risk."

"I can't go with you," Barbara said firmly, wishing she could. "I can't leave my family forever."

"Your decision is final then?"

"Yes."

"Then it will be unlikely that we will ever be able to see each other again."

"Why can't you live here?"

"You know I can't," Mylok said. "My people need me. If you turn me down, I can't ever return here again for the possibility of giving away my world is far too great."

Barbara started to cry, figuring that she would never see Mylok again. Nevertheless, her family came first. She still had her boyfriend, Paul, whom she loved. They had been dating for over two and a half years, and had spoken about getting married upon her graduation. How could she have been so cruel to Paul by seeing Mylok, she wondered? She realized how much Paul meant to her. Barbara wanted to spend the rest of her life with him.

Barbara sat Mylok down to explain herself to him. Barbara wanted to live her own life. More than that, she needed to earn what she got from life. One day, she would buy her own house and settle down with Paul to raise a family. She would soon graduate as an astronomer and pursue her career. Her life of total freedom was ahead of her next year. This is how Barbara wanted to spend the remaining years of her life, even though she knew she would miss Mylok very much.

The possibility of Barbara bringing her friends and family to Mylok's world was out of the question for the harm it could cause. He risked his entire world coming to her. Mylok could never tell Barbara the fate of her world. The aliens forbid him to tamper with the earth's destiny. She believed that with global warming, the devastation of the rain forests, over population, and the planet's finite resources, her dream of someday having grandchildren may not have much of a future. Nevertheless, there is always hope! Technology may someday avail.

Soon, Barbara thanked Mylok for everything he had done for her: the expensive dinners, the trip to Paris, showing her his home in the Bermuda Triangle, and repairing her car. She then climbed into her car to drive home. With her car loaded up with all of her school things, Barbara left Mylok standing alone in front of her dorm building. Without looking back, Barbara drove off to live her own life, never to see him again.

With his car across the street, Mylok watched as Barbara drove the long trip home. His heart burned with a fire it hadn't known for thousands of years. For the first time since his father's death, a tear came to Mylok's eye.

A week had gone by since Barbara had seen Mylok. Barbara's old boyfriend, Paul, had not called her the entire week. Because of the long commute to work, she had to give up her job of waitressing for the summer. On top of that, the competition for summer employment made it almost impossible for her to find a local job. Barbara hated the daily nagging from her aunt and uncle to search for a job.

Pressure at home became more unbearable. Sharing her old bedroom with her younger cousins started to drive Barbara crazy. They never gave her privacy and were always taking her things. She was never able to watch any of her TV shows because of her two male cousins. To make things more unbearable, all of Barbara's friends lived too far away to visit. Also, her uncle would yell at her for staying on the phone too long while talking to Roo, Patty, or Debra. Barbara's loneliness ate away at her body each day.

Soon, the lonely weekend dragged on by. Paul had not called Barbara for their usual Saturday night date. Barbara became concerned since it was not like him not to call.

By Tuesday night, Barbara finally decided to call Paul. She learned that Paul was very upset that she was ever with Mylok. Paul believed that Barbara had dumped him and now he wanted never to see her again.

As the days passed, Barbara called Paul several times. She told Paul how sorry she was for her behavior. Paul even went as far as to take Barbara on a routine date. However, their relationship did not seem the same. The long commute from home only allowed the couple to see each other once a week. Paul had a full-time job as a gas attendant during the week. Not to mention, he did not have a car to visit her.

Barbara believed him to be dating another girl on the side. Paul's new girlfriend, Sylvia, lived not far from him. They started to see each other about every night, Barbara thought. Due to the summer vacation, Barbara knew she was starting to lose Paul to Sylvia. Weekends soon passed by without his ever calling her. Barbara figured he was spending his Saturday nights with his new girlfriend.

Over the weeks, Barbara knew that she had not only given up Mylok, but was starting to lose Paul as well. She laid in bed thinking of what Mylok had once told her. Mylok was right all along. Barbara had no life worth living where she was. A person struggles her entire life in the hopes of making money so that she can someday enjoy life to the fullest. She wanted to do the things worth living for. Mylok had given that to her, and she threw it away. Never again would she see him or have that opportunity.

Barbara wished to do things she had never done before. Though she loved Paul deeply, her body yearned for a change. Barbara did not wish to spend the rest of her life doing the same thing week after week. Many times, Barbara had turned down dates, due to her relationship with Paul. However, each time she turned down a date, the feeling of excitement for something new and different slowly ate away at her body. Mylok seemed to be her fantasy man come true.

Paul was a partier, and he barely graduated high school. So, how could he amount to much in life? He seldom held a good steady job. How could Paul support a family as a gas attendant? He could not! Paul had enough troubles supporting himself. The future was uncertain. How could her marriage with Paul work out?

Paul was the only boy she really knew. Barbara still remembered meeting Paul her freshman year at the university. Due to her over protective uncle, Paul was her first real boyfriend. After two and a half years of dating, their rela-tionship became boring; dead conversations, dinner and movie weekends were all she had to look forward to. It was too routine! Where's the excitement in life? Roo had many boyfriends and had something exciting going on all the time. Roo has been to many new places. Like her nickname implied, she was always on the hop, just like a kangaroo. There was no change in Barbara's life. Barbara remembered the great conversations with Mylok, and he had given her the best excitement in her life. She soon realized, that she was falling in love with Mylok! Barbara soon cried herself to sleep.

It was not until late morning that Barbara woke up. Her pillow was still wet from her tears. She then decided to have a hot bath to help relax. As she soaked her body in the tub, the memory of seeing herself as a young girl on Mylok's screen emerged in her mind. Again her thoughts of him upset her.

Barbara laid in the cooling water for over an hour wondering how she could possibly reach him in the Bermuda Triangle. It was impossible. How could she get miles beneath the ocean to visit him? Again, she started to cry. She cried out to him, "Mylok, I'm sorry."

As the time passed by, Barbara knew she had to forget Paul and Mylok, or she would not be able to function. She figured that music would help her forget her troubles. While relaxing in her bedroom, Barbara decided to look among her many CDs. Then, she found one of her favorite CDs. Barbara placed her CD in the small stereo system she had brought back from school, and she listened to the music of Barry Manilow.

While laying in bed, Barbara heard a knock on her bedroom door. "Come in," she said, leaping from her bed to turn down the CD player.

The door opened and a head emerged. "Hey, I'm taking a ride to the store," cousin Glen said. "Would you like me to pick up something for you?"

"No thanks," Barbara sniffed, while thinking of the times with Mylok. "I'm all set."

"Later then," cousin Glen said, while looking at Barbara. He was like a very close brother to her. Cousin Glen then noted her sadness and added affectionately, "Hey, Barbarian. You OK."

"I was just thinking of Grandpa," she lied. The truth about Mylok was out of the question.

"Yeah. Nursing homes depress me too," cousin Glen laughed, trying to figure out Barbara's loose emotions.

"No. Chicago Grandpa," she said correcting him. Cousin Glen then realized that she was referring to the one that past away.

Cousin Glen then entered the room with a guilty look on his face. "I remember stealing a ball out of his bedroom the week before he died," he stated. "I find it hard to believe that it still bothers me at times."

A ball! Barbara thought. Could this of been Mylok's missing orb? "Was this ball the size of a baseball?" Barbara asked. "Was it pearl-like? Did it glow?"

"Yeah. How did you know?"

"My god, Glen! Do you know what you've done!"

"Who gives a damn."

"Where's the orb?" Barbara said with a slip of the lip. "What have you done with it?"

"How the hell should I know," he replied. "I was like five years old."

"Glen, it's important that you tell me everything you can about the ball," Barbara said, while shaking him. "How did you find it?"

"For a couple of nights, it was like it called to me in my dreams, and I found it in his bedroom the next day," cousin Glen said in disbelief. During the visit, he slept in the room closest to their grandfather's bedroom.

"Where is it?"

"Beats the hell out of me."

"Glen!" she screamed.

"I don't know, Barbarian," cousin Glen replied in anger. He truly did not remember, and why all this fuss over a stupid ball. "Well, I'm out of here," he said, referring to his trip to the store. "You're really nuts kid," he added, while slamming the bedroom door behind him.

Barbara had to get the news of the missing orb to Mylok. As she listened to the music, Barbara remembered hearing the song that night in Mylok's apartment. Suddenly, she found the solution to getting in touch with Mylok. Barbara remembered the doorway into his world through the teleporting doorway within his bedroom closet. How could she have forgotten?

"I won't be home for dinner," Barbara told her aunt, as she raced out the front door. Then, Barbara jumped into her car and drove toward his apartment. She knew that it would be a long trip to get there; at least three hours and twenty minutes. The only hope she had was if she could remember the exact location of his apartment building. It was night time when Mylok had brought her to his place, and he had been driving.

Unfortunately, Barbara had never been to his part of town before. She knew she was too shook up that night to remember exactly where he lived. She recalled that it was not too far from the restaurant that they had gone to on their first date. Barbara knew how to get to the restaurant. It was not that far from the university. Mylok's apartment had to be found. It was her only hope of ever reaching Mylok again. She had to try!

While in the fast lane, Barbara's enthusiasm to be with Mylok caused her to speed fifteen miles over the speed limit. The police pulled her over. The burning sensation of waiting seemed unbearable to her, as the police officer wrote up the speeding ticket. Thanks to the cop, she felt that fifteen minutes to be spent with Mylok had just been wasted. Barbara had no trouble reaching the restaurant. The hard thing now was to try to find his apartment building.

With some luck, Barbara managed to find the apartment building without much trouble. It felt to her as though a strange force had led her there. She sensed that hope was near.

The wait for the elevator seemed endless. The apartment was on the fourteenth floor. Barbara remembered pushing that button herself after asking Mylok the floor number. Even though she could not recall the exact apartment number, there was no doubt in her mind of his apartment being on the corner. It was off toward the side of the elevator.

As the elevator door opened, Barbara raced toward his apartment. She had found it at last. She was finally going to see Mylok. After peeping through the peep hole, she realized that she could not see into the room. It looked black inside. She pounded on the door, and started to call out in the hope that he would hear her. Barbara continued to pound on the door. Yet there was no answer. Fifteen minutes had passed when she screamed his name out for the last time: "MYLOK!"

Barbara did not give up. She knew that Mylok could probably not hear her screaming if he was in his world in the Bermuda Triangle. If his bedroom and closet doors were closed, then he wouldn't hear her. Waiting for him was the only solution, she thought. If he was out for the night, eventually he would have to come back.

Barbara sat in front of the door to wait for him. Occasionally, she would pound the back of her head in the desperate hope that she would be heard by him. She waited a couple of hours, pacing up and down the hallway. Every time the elevator stopped on that floor, she would run to see if it was him. Nevertheless, it was not.

Then she frantically pounded on the door and shouted his name. A couple coming off the elevator watched her from behind.

"Can I help you, Miss?" the man asked Barbara.

"No," Barbara replied, blushing over how crazy she must look to them. "I'm just waiting for my boyfriend. He should be here any time now."

"I'm afraid he moved three months ago," the helpful gentleman told her.

"Three months ago?" Barbara asked in a confused state. "I was here no more than five weeks ago."

"Are you sure you have the right floor?" the stranger asked. His date started to get impatient with him.

"I'm positive," Barbara exclaimed without a doubt in her mind. "I remember seeing this stain on the rug last time I was here. You must have seen Mylok."

"I'm afraid that no one by that name ever lived there," the short, hefty man told her as he opened his apartment door across the hall. "The Lymans were the last to live there. That apartment has been vacant for at least three months." Barbara looked into the man's apartment and noticed that it was the exact opposite of Mylok's. The man with his date had then entered into his apartment.

"Could you please call the manager for me?" Barbara asked him as he was about to close the door in her face.

"It's empty."

"Please," Barbara begged.

"All right," the man responded reluctantly, wishing that he had never gotten involved with her. "You will have to take full responsibility."

"Sure," Barbara told him as he closed the door behind him.

Minutes passed. Barbara began to feel like a fool. She figured that the man had never made the call. She had the urge to tell him off. However, before she knocked on the stranger's door, a well dressed man approached her. The manager of the building said, "I had a phone call of someone needing assistance."

"That was me," Barbara told the manager.

"What seems to be the trouble?"

"I can't get into the apartment."

"Does this apartment belong to you?"

"No." Barbara hesitated. "I heard that this apartment is vacant. I was hoping that you could show me around." She figured that a little white lie would be the only way he would open the door for her.

The manager felt as though he could not stick to formalities with someone who may be a potential renter. He opened the door with his pass key. The room was pitch black. The manager reached around the corner with his hand and flipped on the light switch. Except for the rug and the curtains to the balcony, the room was completely empty.

Barbara's hopes diminished at the sight of the empty room. Barbara knew she would be in big trouble if she did not think quickly. "Mind if I check the bedroom?"

"Please do," the hopeful manager said.

"I'll be just a minute."

"Take your time."

Barbara ran into the bedroom. She slid her arm along the wall in search of the light switch. The bright overhead light flicked on after she hit the switch. She lunged toward the closet door. As Barbara grabbed the handle of the sliding door, her hand was trembling. "Please!" she screamed to herself for some hope, as she slid the door open. However, the closet was empty.

month had passed. Barbara often cried herself to sleep at night. There was no way she would ever see Mylok again. Barbara could not handle that reality. Losing Paul and Mylok led to her great depression.

Barbara was now back for her senior year at the university. All of her time was spent on her studies. She even got her old job back as a waitress. On several occasions, Barbara would mistake a customer's voice for Mylok's. Working there made it more difficult to forget him.

After losing both Paul and Mylok, she did not ever want to date another man. Barbara had been hurt too badly. Although men had asked her out, she turned them all down. She always made up a story so that she would not feel obligated to accept any of their offers. Possibly, it was that she was just too drained from both work and her studies to handle a relationship at this time.

Again, Barbara lived with her old roommate, Roo. However, Barbara would sometimes take her anger out on innocent Roo. At times, Barbara came close to losing the only friend she had left. Like a fish in its own little bowl, Barbara began to withdraw in her own world. Occasionally, she would snap at people, especially males. Barbara would not even party as she used to. Most of her time had to be spent on study and work. Last year, Barbara had decided to major in computer science as well as astronomy. She knew senior year was going to be her toughest yet.

Early one morning, Barbara was particularly busy at the restaurant. One of the waitresses was sick, thus placing a heavier load on the remaining three waitresses, including Barbara. Nonetheless, she stayed calm and relaxed as she bounced from table to table. Many of the customers were becoming impatient with her because she was making them late for work. From every table in her section, it seemed that someone was constantly requesting something. It did not upset her though. Barbara knew she was only human.

"How about some service?" a young executive asked politely.

"I'll be right with you," Barbara told him with her back turned as she continued waiting on another table.

"I'm in no rush," the considerate man said. "I understand. You're only human." Barbara smiled for the first time in weeks. His understanding just made her whole day.

"What can I get you?" Barbara asked of the well dressed man as she turned around to take his order.

"You."

Barbara stared at the wise guy, figuring another one was trying to ask her for a date. Nonetheless, his voice sounded familiar. As she looked at him, her mind suddenly registered who he was. "Mylok!"

"I just happened to be flying over America and decided to drop in to say hello," Mylok said with a smile.

"I thought I would never see you again," Barbara said, her heart filled with joy.

"I didn't expect to see you," Mylok exclaimed. "Your people have a saying, 'Rules are made to be broken.' I had to see you again." Mylok's love for her was too great. Against his better judgment, Mylok risked the fate of his people. With a smile on his face, he added, "I decided to up my chances of your accepting my proposal to the best two out of three."

"I can't accept your proposal to live with you," she told him, understanding what he had meant by his words. Mylok was giving her a second chance to live with him in his world.

"I was going to offer you a chance to visit me for a couple of days," he cajoled her.

"You knew all along that I wanted to see you again," she said coldly. "You've been watching me through the Tzorb, haven't you?" Mylok nodded his head, admitting that she knew him well. It was the only reason why he was permitted his priests blessings to come back to her. "I had hoped you would," she said.

"You're ready to leave now then?"

"I can't take two days off from work," Barbara explained, "I'll lose my job."

"Your boss wouldn't mind, especially if you can get Sue to back you up for those days." Mylok said persuasively. Due to the Tzorb's aid, Mylok already knew that the name of one of the other girls who work with Barbara was Sue. In addition, Sue was looking for extra hours.

"What am I going to tell him?"

"Tell him there has been a family tragedy."

"You're sneaky," Barbara told him. "I think it may work." Barbara had to be with Mylok again. She had missed him so much. However, she did not wish to jeopardize her job because of it. Barbara decided to try it. She left Mylok to speak with her boss and Sue. Mylok's plan worked.

"We'd like some service," a businessperson called out. Her manager started to look at Barbara with concern for his customers.

"Sorry," Barbara replied to the impatient man. "I'm off duty." Mylok had stood up from the chair to help escort her outside. Turning to her boss, she told him, "Thanks again."

"I'll see you on Thursday!" the manager said. She then walked out of the restaurant, clinging to Mylok's arm.

Without looking back, Barbara willingly traveled with Mylok to the Bermuda Triangle. Mylok kept his promise. He was now going to show her a world which she never could have imagined. Barbara and he walked through his diverse rooms. Each one was a unique representation of different nations and centuries. Each one, the size of a palace room, was breathtaking in its own right.

Mylok brought her back to the Tzorb room. Barbara told Mylok about the news that her cousin Glen had told her. Mylok kept his promise and showed her his vast world on the giant screen. A world beneath the earth's crust. Upon the screen, she saw three tall, thin buildings, each of which with a dome on top of alien glass.

Mylok explained to her, "Each of these three towers are approximately one square mile in base. The towers taper at the top, which measures slightly over three-quarters of a mile." While Mylok spoke, the screen gave the measurements along the sides of the towers like an electronic blueprint.

"Then we're twelve miles down from where we parked the car," Barbara mused.

"Yes."

"You live on the top floor," she said. "Which tower?" Barbara asked, looking at the diagram upon the large screen.

"I live on the top two floors of all three towers," Mylok told her.

"How is that possible?" she asked. "The other towers are five miles away. How do you get to them?"

"The teleporting doorways combine the three towers into one structure," Mylok explained.

"That's fascinating! How have you developed such technology?" Barbara asked.

"Modern man couldn't," Mylok said. "Only with the aid of an alien world far superior to ours was it possible. The windows of the towers are of the same crystal glass that prevents the molten lava from consuming the buildings."

"How is it possible to build such tall buildings without having them topple?"

"The molten rock acts much like the buoyancy of water," Mylok said. "It can support the weight of the buildings. The metallic structure can be supported above ground as well. The metal used here in construction is lighter and stronger than anything employed in your world."

"If the buildings are floating in the lava, what keeps them from floating off somewhere else?" Barbara asked.

"Don't worry. They're not going anywhere," Mylok laughed. "The towers are anchored to the Tzorb."

Barbara thought to herself for a second. Then, she said aloud, "If the towers have a base of one mile each, and they are five miles apart, then the Tzorb would have to be close to seven miles wide."

"It's thirty-two cubic miles."

"Wow!" she said. "What is the need for such a large computer?"

"I told you before, Barbara. The Tzorb is not a computer," Mylok said refreshing her memory. "The Tzorb gets its energy from the earth's thermal heat. This is much like the sun's solar energy. However, this source is far superior."

"The sun is larger than the earth," Barbara exclaimed. "The sun has greater energy."

"Yes. However, the sun loses its energy from being so far away from the earth," Mylok told her. "The earth is like having the sun right here. Its energy is far greater, due to the convenience of processing it. In response to her previous question, Mylok continued, "The Tzorb gives us our life support systems. You can call it the brain of the world. The Tzorb knows everything about this earth. It knows of every man's actions since his birth. It has counted every grain of sand down to its last atom for the past five thousand years."

"How can the Tzorb store such information?"

"It can't," Mylok said. "Everything is stored in the earth's radiating energy."

"You make it sound like the earth is a thinking computer," Barbara said, giving Mylok a bizarre look.

"The earth is a living entity just like you and me."

"Please, don't kid me," she said.

"A killer whale has a brain much larger than man's," Mylok responded, stating a fact that Barbara already knew. "The killer whale is also far superior in intellect to man. You see the whale as only being a stupid fish. What has it ever accomplished? It could never achieve the things man has. It doesn't need to. On the other hand, man could never tell of his life story in one word as the whale can. The intellectual superiority of many underwater creatures is the result of their longer evolutionary scale. You can't call something non intelligent just because you don't understand it."

"So the killer whale is smarter than man," Barbara stated. "I've never heard the world speaking to me."

"I'm sure you never tried to listen before."

"This is silly," Barbara chuckled. "You really expect me to believe the earth is alive and thinking."

"Yes, just like the bacteria on your eyelashes," Mylok reminded her. "We too, are nothing more than bacteria living on the earth. A fly's life is but a few days. A man's life can average over seventy years. Certain species of trees live for centuries."

"What are you getting at?" Barbara asked.

"We both know the earth is five billion years old," Mylok continued. "It has a life that is evolutionary, but constant. By looking at a snail for a few seconds, we would think that it is dead due to its lack of motion. It does not speak to you or engage in fast movement. Yet, we know that the snail is alive," Mylok said, looking at her. "Life is nothing more than living energy."

"A planet is nothing more than a sun that has cooled down," Barbara quoted from her astronomy courses. "You're saying that the sun is also a living thing."

"A sun and planet live and die," Mylok continued. "They reproduce with the joining of others and speak in patterns of light unknown to your world. Planets and stars can communicate with one another with this type of telepathic light energy. Their language is not heard by your world and is therefore overlooked."

Barbara listened for hours while asking Mylok hundreds of questions about his world. She then asked him, "Then you're the only person who has access to the Tzorb. Why is that?"

"I am the 'Keeper' of the Tzorb, hence the title, Mylok." he stated. My real name is Malik. I have been chosen by the aliens to watch the world from a non-biased view point. All information learned in this world is relayed back to neighboring worlds in exchange for their knowledge and aid. Then, the people of the earth are able to advance in their technology."

"I'm afraid I don't understand what you're talking about."

"It is my world that led your people to where they are today," Mylok said. "My people are the students of our alien teachers."

"How can that be?"

"The aliens were unable to communicate to the people in words," Mylok continued. "They communicated to a few through telepathy. However, any person using his telepathy with one of them was only able to understand pictures of thoughts. These images became the characters of our alphabet. This was how our writing of hieroglyphics developed."

"That would explain the picture writing and carvings of the ancient times," Barbara replied.

"The aliens' teachings showed us a system of counting by tens based upon the number of fingers on our hands. Their counting system counts by twelves, due to their six fingers on each hand."

"You're kidding." Barbara asked him, "How is it possible to count by twelves?"

"It is possible to count by any number," Mylok replied. "Your modern computer field has systems that count by two, eight, and sixteen."

"You're right," Barbara admitted. "They're known as the binary, octal, and hexadecimal counting systems. I recall that from my computer courses at the university. The octal system of counting by eights was extremely important for programming on the PDP-11 series computer."

"This counting by tens later became the foundations of your modern day arithmetic and geometry," he said, while flashing more pictures on the large screen of the space travelers aiding his people. "With their wisdom, the aliens helped us pioneer the field of astronomy. They showed a few of our selected scientists how to distinguish between the planets and stars. This enabled us to devise our 365-day calendar."

"Wow," she said at a loss of words.

"They also showed us how to mine the earth for its precious metals," Mylok said to bedazzle her. "The invention of glass was achieved by purifying sand. Believe me, we had plenty of that."

Barbara laughed at his quick wit, knowing that most of Egypt was in the desert. She asked, "What else?"

"They helped our people by showing them how to irrigate our crops," Mylok said. "Also how to take advantage of the flooding season of the Nile River." Mylok flashed pictures of some rulers of the ancient past on the screen. He said, "My people developed the world's first national government. All this was due to the help of a life form higher than ours."

"The aliens," she said knowingly. "What else have the aliens taught the Egyptians?"

"They showed us new medicines and surgical techniques. Even today, your people can't explain our process of mummification."

"That would also explain how the blocks of the pyramids fit together within a hundredth of an inch," she added. "Nobody could figure out how they had been built. We don't even have the capabilities to do so today."

"Correct."

"Why were the pyramids built?" Asked Barbara. "Were they just tombs?"

"In part," Mylok explained. "They are much more! The pyramids along with the Nile River map out the star constellation of Orion. The Orion system is the home system of our alien visitors and a message to the people of earth. When your technology comes to the point of galactic travel, the pyramids mark an invitation for space travel.

"What did they get out of all of this?"

The Tzorb then showed her the answer. People being slain for their lack of loyalty. "In exchange, we worshiped them like gods," Mylok replied to her. "We believed them to be gods. We gave them offerings and sacrifices in exchange for their knowledge. Many of the sacrifices were even human."

"Yuck," Barbara said as she shuddered at the picture on the screen. The beating heart of a man had been cut from his opened chest. "That's terrible...now just a minute. That doesn't look Egyptian. It looks more like Aztec."

"You're correct," Mylok explained. "The points of our four orbs were also points of predominant alien contact. At least they showed the people that there is life after death."

"I still find that hard to believe," Barbara said. She then asked Mylok, "Why is it hard for me to believe in that?"

"Your internal energy is enclosed within yourself as is your mind," Mylok answered her. He then continued with his philosophical lecture, "Life as a human is much like the flow of water. It is neither a gas nor a solid. When a person dies, his heavenly spirit is transformed, much like the water changing to gas. Only then is the spirit able to fly and reach out like the steam of boiling water. However, if the soul is evil it becomes trapped within itself, much like the ice cube is unable to travel outward due to its enclosed state."

"Then, I must be an ice cube trapped within myself," Barbara told Mylok.

"Don't worry," Mylok said as he wrapped his arm around her. He then kissed her from the side. "I'll heat you up."

"That you can," she said with a smile. "I always feared death."

"My people are not afraid to die," Mylok said. "Death is nothing to be feared. It is only a metamorphosis of soul from body like that of the butterfly from the caterpillar. Death is nothing more than a peaceful dream. A person does not fear sleep."

"So there is life after death?"

"Absolutely," Mylok said. "Like the caterpillar, you can consider your life a preschool before the afterlife. One doesn't truly live until after death. Though, death is an illusion."

"Death is quite real. How can you say it's an illusion?"

"Like the planets around our sun, so too, are the electrons around a proton," Mylok explained. "Therefore, the field of quantum psychics dictates that your body is ninety-nine point nine percent empty space. The illusion is that you believe that you are a being of matter. Whereas, you are held together by energy. You are an energy being! Energy can only be transformed--never destroyed. The fact is, be trying to destroy energy you get more energy. The theory of an atomic bomb shows that."

"Is there a god?"

"God is the universal energy force that unites all creation. Energy is an ocean of intelligence."

"If everything is composed of atoms, than everything would be an ocean of pure energy."

"Yes, every person, every animal, every plant, to a rock, to the ever lasting universe, are all one!" Mylok stated. "During a year, your entire body is just about composed of new atoms only maintaining your form through intelligence."

"Wow, that's incredible," she said, while pausing in awe.

Hours passed by as Barbara learned a little more about herself and the Mylokian world. With the aid of the Tzorb, they searched for the missing Orb of Sun-God Ra. Mylok now knew that cousin Glen was the key. However, on this day, luck was not on their side.

In failure of finding the orb, they left the Tzorb and shared an enjoyable lunch. Again, Barbara met Mylok's pet, Maxalavar. Barbara called him Max for short. Max did many tricks for her. While singing in his native language, Max entranced her with a song and dance. As Mylok played his ancient instrument, Max balanced himself on his long, strong tail. Maxalavar flipped in the air several times and bedazzled her with his fancy footwork. While bouncing among the furniture in the master bedroom, Max sang an old Egyptian song.

Barbara had much fun watching them perform. Soon, Mylok programmed the Tzorb so that old Egyptian songs engulfed the room. The central computer played his requests upon the stereo system hidden within his bedroom. The three laughed together as they all danced to the ancient music.

"Time to get back to work," Mylok said, breaking up their party. She knew he was a very busy man. Perhaps the busiest in the world. An overlord could not keep a world together by playing around all day. Barbara knew he worked hard while she slept through the night. Mylok confessed to her that he would go back to work as she slept. He never slept!

Mylok only needed to meditate for twenty minutes a day. Often times, she believed he did not even require that.

"Place these in your ears," Mylok said.

"Why?"

"They are translation devices," he replied. "These ear plugs will translate any foreign language so that you can understand it. Today you will meet many new people at work creating new things and ideas. With these, you will be able to understand what they're discussing. Unfortunately, they won't be able to understand you since none of them speaks English."

"These will enable me to hear and even understand Egyptian?" she asked while snugly fitting them into her ears.

"I asked you before not to repeat that word, 'Egyptian' or even mention Egypt," Mylok reminded her scoldingly. "It is, considered an insult to these people. The Egyptians were a very primitive people compared to us."

"Sorry," she said. "Then what should I call your people?"

"They refer to themselves as Mylok-savar--followers of Mylok," he insisted. That's right, Barbara thought. She knew that. Mylok was the ruler of his people. Barbara kept forgetting that, because he didn't act like any ruler she ever recalled from her history lessons. He seemed and acted much as a middle-class person would. Mylok never had any servants fussing over him.

Mylok took her throughout many of his people's scientific laboratories. Here, she met many of Mylok's friends. He treated his people as friends, not as subjects of his kingdom.

It seemed peculiar to Barbara, hearing Mylok's people speak English since their lips never matched the words spoken. What seemed even more strange was that a person would stop speaking, but she continued to hear the translation. Barbara wondered how such a small device was able to match each person's voice pattern. Any computerized device that she was aware of had only one fixed voice tone. However, Barbara was still unable to understand some words because they were not yet invented in her world.

Mylok acted much like the president of his own company. He traveled throughout his many departments asking and answering many questions.

His replies were always helpful. It seemed that his ideas contained great depth.

Barbara soon realized that Mylok was not the master of only one particular field but of hundreds. Barbara believed that Mylok had accumulated the knowledge equivalent to a PhD degree in every subject offered at her university. She suddenly realized the power of the Tzorb traveling through him. Mylok actually did know all that existed!

Mylok was also in control of the towers' life support systems. Barbara saw the enormous power plants manufactured by the earth's molten energy. She soon understood the superiority of the energy generated from the heat of the earth's molten core compared to that of nuclear energy. All the real energy was contained within the center of a star. That also included the earth, which was only a star operating at a cooler temperature.

Mylok had explained the energy process, but she did not fully understand it yet. It would take time to adapt to this new world and culture.

Her two day visit quickly passed. Barbara had seen but a fraction of the whole Mylokian world. There was still so much more to experience. However, it was time to head back home. Barbara knew she was falling behind in her studies and had to get back to work. "I had a great time seeing you again, Mylok," Barbara told him with joy. "I think it's time that I head back home."

"From now on, your home shall be with my people," Mylok exclaimed with sorrow for her. Mylok knew that she could never return to her world ever again.

"This is no time to be joking. I would like you to take me home now," she demanded of him.

"Barbara, for your own protection, you shall spend the rest of your life living the Mylokian way," he said firmly.

"Are you serious?"

"I'm very serious, Barbara."

"You're kidnaping me?" she asked. This had to be a bad joke. As Mylok nodded his head, confirming that it was true, Barbara started to become hysterical. She screamed at him. No longer would she be able to see her family and friends. Like many of the other people who passed through the Bermuda Triangle from the outside world, Barbara would forever disappear. "You lied to me! I hate you!" she screamed again, as she lunged at Mylok to claw out his eyes with her long fingernails.

"I'm sorry that it has to be this way," Mylok said while trapping her arms. She screamed frantically and struggled to get away from his strong grip. Then, she kneed him in the leg, while missing her target by two inches. "If I could let you go home, I would," Mylok told her. "Now you need rest. I'll see you soon."

"Why are you doing this to me? I want to go home!" Barbara screamed, as Mylok left the room.

Mylok left her to rest on his energy field bed. Barbara quickly thought of escaping from the Bermuda Triangle. The only means of escape that she knew of was Mylok's car or the teleporting doorways. Realizing from experience that she could not operate either of these without Mylok's fingerprint authorization, Barbara knew she was trapped in the room. Deep down, she did not want to leave Mylok. She loved him. Barbara also believed that he felt the same for her. In the past, he had never tried to hurt her, and he seemed sincere about letting her go home--if he could. Mylok had to be doing this for some good reason, she thought. Possibly, her knowing too much about his world to be trusted outside of the Bermuda Triangle was the problem.

Barbara slowly had to blend into her new world. She cried for days, unable to forget her family and friends back in America. Mylok had canceled Tzorb access through the computer to Barbara. Soon, Barbara learned more words of the Mylokian language to keep her from getting bored the many hours Mylok was away for work. Barbara had run out of things to break! Time was all she had left to her.

Hours at a time were spent using the computer in Mylok's bedroom to learn the more advanced form of hieroglyphics. As Mylok worked, he would leave her to study his language. The computer made it easy to learn just a few words through the English spelling. Unfortunately, many of the words spoken could not be deciphered in the English language because of their foreign pronunciations. Barbara felt as though she was again in the first grade trying to learn her ABC's.

One day, Mylok approached her from behind. Barbara was having difficulty memorizing the first 32 Egyptian type characters of the Mylokian alphabet. She practiced writing the symbols on the table's screen with her computer pen. "Having trouble?" he asked.

"No, I've got these all memorized," she lied, quickly deleting the writing table. Barbara did not want him to see how terrible she was at duplicating the symbols.

"Good," Mylok said. "You'll now be able to continue onto the next set of characters," Mylok added, sensing her dishonesty. "Our alphabet alone has slightly over 700 letters in it." On the large central screen within the wall, Mylok flashed the entire alphabet of characters.

Barbara wanted to abandon her studies forever after hearing that. Only a few of the advanced hieroglyphics were comprehensible to her. In addition, writing the symbols just added to her aggravation. An artist she was not.

"You look bewildered," Mylok stated.

"You had to be on an acid trip to have designed an alphabet as wild as that," she said despairingly. "Time to relax," he told her. "How about a game of tennis?"

"Sure, I could use the exercise," Barbara said sluggishly. The two walked through the teleporting doorway and into a long hallway. Most of the walls were covered with the writings of deceased people's past lives. It was much like memorial scriptures in memory of their achievements. She still had the habit of looking at the walls as they walked, curious about their meanings.

"In time, you'll be reading the walls to me," Mylok said teasingly as he shook his head at the thought of that day.

Barbara gave him a dirty look to show she understood his sarcastic remark.

"Ready for a good game of four dimensional tennis?" he asked, trying to change the subject as they approached the tennis courts.

"What do you mean 'four dimensional?' There's only three."

"Just that," Mylok replied as they entered into a large room. Several observation windows stood along the sides of the far wall. It sounded to Barbara as though there were several games of racquetball going on at the same time. The couple observed a game in action as they peeked through a wall of thick glass. For the first time, she watched a game of four dimensional tennis. Mylok answered her question, "You see. The game is played in an antigravity room."

Barbara watched a couple playing a game. It was strange to see them returning the ball from standing on the walls and ceiling. It did not seem possible. "How is it that the girl is able to stand on the glass?" Barbara asked as the girl stood on the window in front of her.

"You see," he explained. "Each player is wearing magnetized shoes that enable them to grip the surfaces. Also, the side of the glass is coated with a transparent metallic sheet. It acts like a one-way window. They can't see us, but we can see them play." Mylok continued, "The object is to hit the ball over the net without having it get trapped on your side."

Barbara watched them play. They made it look so easy. The court was about the same size as a typical court back home, but the room was enclosed much as in racquetball. The net was positioned around the room. However, unlike a regular court that has the net on the ground, this tennis net was supported by four cords. Each cord was connected in the center of the "four" floors from the top of the net to the other adjoining playing surfaces. The net traveled along the floor, walls, and the ceiling.

The ball had then landed on the man's side of the net. The ball was lifeless in the net. Barbara knew the woman scored a point. She saw the man retrieve the ball and then float to the ceiling to serve. The tennis ball traveled extremely fast in this antigravity environment. Except for the minute air resistance to slow it down, the tennis ball did not have the restraint of gravity to ever stop it.

"That looks like fun," Barbara said to Mylok. "When can we try it?"

"Right now."

Mylok took her to the dressing room. Hundreds of tennis shoes were lined up along the dressing room wall. Mylok selected them both a pair to wear since Barbara was not yet able to distinguish between the different shoe sizes. The symbols on the back on the shoes confused her.

Next, Mylok chose for her the proper tennis outfit: a pair of socks, blouse, mini skirt, and panties. They were bundled as one package. He selected an outfit for himself in the male section of the outfitting room. Barbara then asked, "Where is the women's dressing room?"

"Here."

"Oh. Then, where is the men's dressing room?"

"Here," he replied, pointing to the same spot.

"You mean that everybody dresses together?" she asked incredulously.

"Yes," Mylok replied as he led her into the locker room. "In this world one is not taught to be embarrassed of one's own body."

"I'm not embarrassed of my body," Barbara retorted as she found an empty locker for her clothes. None of the lockers had doors or a way to lock them. She then asked Mylok, "Can't somebody steal our clothes?"

"Yes," he replied. "What do you have worth taking? I'm sure that no one entered here without their clothes."

She got dressed quickly for fear she would be seen by other people. Barbara knew that she would die if someone entered before she had the chance to cover her naked body. Why couldn't they at least have a front door to the dressing room? She thought.

"Your panties are on backwards," Mylok laughed as he saw her cute fanny hanging out of them. She had been in too great of a rush to realize it. Barbara looked down at them and realized he was right. She quickly reversed them.

Upon entering the antigravity room, Mylok jumped toward the ceiling after retrieving the floating tennis ball. It was obvious that he was a pro at this game. Barbara had a weightless feeling upon entering the room. She laughed as she placed her tennis racket in front of her. The racket just floated, as she fixed the straps on her padded crash helmet. Mylok didn't need one, nor did the couple before them. Barbara felt ridiculous all padded up. Mylok had even made her wear knee and elbow pads.

"The shoes are only attracted to a surface if you are within a foot of it," Mylok said. "Be extremely cautious of jumping or you'll head right for the ceiling. When you jump, tuck your body in and shoot your feet toward the opposite direction like this." Mylok jumped toward the floor near Barbara. He grabbed her around the waist from behind her. "Jump," he commanded.

Together they jumped. She forgot to tuck. Fortunately, Mylok tucked inward, therefore turning them both around. They were now on the ceiling. "You forgot to tuck. Let's try it again," he said.

Barbara thought she was going to lose her lunch after her first jump. It was a good thing they had eaten several hours ago. She was going to be a good sport about this. "I'm ready," she exclaimed. Again they jumped and this time she remembered to tuck.

"Good," Mylok said. "That's it. You're getting the hang of it."

The two of them practiced the basics for a few minutes. Developing skill takes practice, she reminded herself, just like skiing. Mylok continued with the fundamentals of the game. "When you move, try to slide your feet. Don't forget that. If you jump up at the ball, you'll keep going," he stated.

"How about a game?" she asked, suddenly feeling confident. She had been brought up on tennis and used to play with her brothers and sisters as well as Roo.

"I believe it would be better if you learned the basics first," Mylok insisted.

"I'm ready for a game," Barbara exclaimed. "Unless, of course, you're afraid that I'll clobber you."

"All right then, stay here and I'll serve you the ball," he said to her. Mylok kicked off the back wall hard. The force of the jump shot him directly to the opposite side of the playing field. He stayed toward the center of the room, therefore missing the net. Mylok then served a ball to her. He also carried a few extra practice balls in a small bag strapped around his waist.

Barbara missed the return. The ball bounced from the center of her back wall and returned to Mylok's side of the net. The ball bounced off Mylok's back wall and for the second time, shot past her. This time she tried to run at it, forgetting about the lack of gravity. Not only did she miss, but the lack of gravity forced her right into the net.

"It will come around again," Mylok said calmly. She pushed off the net to lunge after the ball. Barbara headed towards a wall head first. At the last second, she stuck out her arms in front of her to cushion the blow.

Barbara landed on her elbows, while bumping her head only slightly. She then realized why Mylok had padded her up so. However, upon hitting the metallic surface, she tried to grab it. Her grabbing action ended up as more of a push. Barbara could only watch as she floated away from the floor. The room seemed hard to comprehend. It had six floors on which she could stand. She successfully landed on the opposite playing wall, this time with her magnetized shoes hitting first. Barbara finally had the support of a surface.

The ball returned to her side again. However, she was now too far away from it. The ball sailed over her head by ten feet. She knew that Mylok had hit that ball only once, but it had returned to her side already four times. Barbara could now hear Mylok chuckling at her. Due to the antigravity, he just floated in the center of the room. He was truly enjoying her comical performance.

Barbara knew she had to get closer to the net to hit the ball or at least stop it. Carefully, she shuffled towards the net, positioning herself in a very wide stance to keep her balance. The inertia of her motion was hard to readjust to. Suddenly, a ball bounced smack between her legs. She stared at it in embarrassment as it continued past her towards Mylok's side. Just then, four other balls also whizzed between her legs. Mylok was laughing himself sick after just setting all of his practice balls into motion.

Due to the lack of gravity within the large room, Mylok now had five tennis balls continuing in an almost spontaneous diamond shaped pattern. If it was not for the air resistance, the balls would have been traveling forever. Each ball went through the net after bouncing off the back walls.

The first ball set into motion by Mylok then hit Barbara in the back. She quickly turned around and grabbed the ball, "I got it!" she screamed.

"The object is not to catch the ball, but to hit it so that it lands within my side of the net," he said as he caught the other flying tennis balls. While holding the racket in his right hand, Mylok quickly grabbed each ball separately with his left hand and placed each within the pouch strapped around his waist. "You can serve this time," he said, now on her side of the playing surface.

Barbara tried to serve the ball as she was accustomed to serving it at home, tossing the ball straight up. Again, she had forgotten the lack of gravity. She cursed to herself, as she watched the ball float away. Barbara had expected the ball to drop back down as her many years of playing had taught her. Instead, the ball quickly hit off the opposite surface and hit her on top of her nose.

"Having trouble?" Mylok asked.

"Yeah. How about some more tennis lessons?" Barbara asked, rubbing her nose. She had to admit it was a much harder game than she had imagined. It was going to be hard for her to break her usual playing habits. For a few more minutes, Mylok reviewed the basics with her.

After their practice session, they walked back to the dressing room. Barbara joined Mylok in undressing. She wanted to fit into her new world, so she decided to copy everything that he did. He soon jumped into the shower with her following right behind. Barbara felt at ease when she saw that no one else was in the shower. She then began to wash herself beside Mylok with her own separate shower head. This feels good, she thought, as she soaked her aching muscles. Barbara was discovering new muscles that she never knew she had.

"Scrub my back and I'll scrub yours," Mylok said to Barbara. Showering together was an old Mylokian tradition.

"That's strange. I've heard that saying before in America many times," she replied as she started scrubbing his back with a sponge cloth.

"That's odd," Mylok said as he drank some of the crystal clear water from the shower head. "I wonder how that saying slipped out of the Bermuda Triangle." Barbara had to think about what he said. She always thought the saying had come from the Japanese, since they had community bath houses. However, it is one sided. Barbara knew that the Japanese women scrub the backs of their men, but she was not sure if the men reciprocated. She then asked, "Are you serious?"

"Yes," he replied as he turned around to rinse off his back. "It's a rather common expression."

"I always thought that saying seemed out of place," she exclaimed as she turned around from Mylok's circular hand gesture. While Mylok scrubbed her back with some liquid soap and a sponge cloth, a couple of men entered the showers with them. The nude men exchanged a casual hello in their native language with Mylok and Barbara as they walked by. As the sweating men turned on their shower heads, Barbara soon felt very self conscious. She did not have a towel with which to cover her naked body.

"Where are you going?" Mylok asked Barbara as she walked out of the shower room with her back lathered up with soap.

"I'm going to die," she replied, blushing at having been seen naked by male strangers.

Chapter 10

Barbara's understanding of the Mylokian language blossomed with each passing day. Maxalavar would often aid Barbara in her studies of the Mylokian language. Max spoke fluent Mylokian, so Barbara thought it was only fair to teach Max some English in return. It seemed to her that Max's understanding of English developed more quickly than her understanding of the Mylokian language. Max seemed to have a photographic memory. Barbara usually had to say a sentence only once and Max would be able to repeat it back to her. He also remembered things more easily than she did. Barbara realized that Mylok hadn't been joking the day he said that Maxalavar had an IQ of 182.

Barbara was extremely frustrated at being unable to pronounce even the most common Mylokian words. The Mylokian language was much more complicated than the English language, Max once admitted to Barbara. Their basic alphabet alone has slightly over 700 characters. The rest of the alphabet was used by the Mylokian scientists only.

"Try it again, beautiful," the helpful dwarf told Barbara. Max rested his head on his tail, as most people would rest their head on a hand. She tried the word again. As Max nodded his head, he winked an eye at Barbara, reassuring her that she had pronounced the troublesome word perfectly.

Barbara made many new friends. During her stay, Barbara must have seen a million people within the confines of the three towers. The towers had hundreds of recreational parks. There were plants from every part of the earth, including some from other worlds. Even though everything was foreign to her, she still found herself wanting to spend the rest of her life in Mylok's world.

Every day, there were new activities for her to explore. Not that it was all fun! Barbara also worked harder than ever before learning Mylok's language. Several of the scientists even gave her some small jobs to do to aid in their research of finding the missing orb. However, she found her work enjoyable and greatly varied. It was the Mylokian way. Boredom and lack of self worth were unknown in this world. Self worth was plentiful for all of Mylok's people. Also, there was plenty of food, shelter, energy, and clothing for all. Hunger, unemployment, and taxes were not a part of this new world. Education was free and greatly respected by the Mylokian people.

Each day meant a potential new breakthrough in technology. Illness was unknown in this world because everyone lived in a germ free environment. She soon realized that they even had a cure for the common cold and AIDS. This advanced world could even eliminate any discovered cancer cells within a person without surgery. The Mylokian technology surpassed the outside world's by thousands of years.

However fun filled this world seemed, Barbara's memories were bound to come back to haunt her eventually. She still missed her family and Roo very much. She figured that her aunt and uncle must think that she was dead. Nobody knew where she had gone. Barbara then remembered the Tzorb. Mylok had not taken her to the computer center for months. He would go by himself, as she stayed to study his language in their bedroom.

One day, Mylok was about to go to the Tzorb room by himself. Barbara swung around in her chair from her studies and asked him, "Where are you off to?"

"The Tzorb."

"I'd like to come with you this time."

"Why?"

"I'd like to see what my parents are up to, if it is all right."

"Barbara," Mylok said to her with sorrow. "The earth above is no longer the same as you once knew it."

"I don't understand what you're talking about," she replied, fearing something was terribly wrong. Mylok never told her the entire truth of why she was taken to his world. Barbara always assumed that it was because she knew too much of his people.

"A few days ago the world was struck by a massive asteroid," Mylok exclaimed. "Eighty-three percent of the world that you knew has been destroyed. Because of the nuclear winter, the little that remains above will also perish. Remember the day I told you I took the Orb of Body from the Louvre museum in Paris? I never told you that the pyramids are also a repelling station from life-threatening asteroids that may collide with earth. The asteroids colliding with Jupiter in 1995 were just a reminder of the dangers of the removal of the third orb. The removal of the two orbs by your archaeologists brought doom to this planet on December 21. As foreseen on that day, the constellation of your solar system did align in the formation of the cross as recorded in your scriptures--The Bible. The curse of King Tut was not a curse! It was a warning of the rapture and destruction of earth!"

"How could you let this happen to the earth?" Barbara cried.

"The damage your people caused from grave robbing made the earth's destruction inevitable," Mylok replied.

"Are you saying that my entire family is dead?" she asked, trying to understand what he was explaining.

"Yes," Mylok stated. Barbara cried uncontrollably, while Mylok held her tight. After a few minutes of comforting her, he said, "You would have also died with them, if you went home that day."

"Oh my god," she said. "You saved my life."

"The choice of life was yours alone," Mylok said.

Barbara was just glad to be alive. "Nothing will survive?"

"The world is covered by a nuclear atmosphere," Mylok stated. "The black clouds no longer allow the sun to warm the earth. All plants and trees will soon die."

"If they die, so too will the rest of the people."

"Correct."

"Won't anybody survive?" she asked.

"The few that survive in fallout shelters will run out of food before the earth can heal its wound."

"Your right," Barbara said. "It took the earth millions of years to develop an atmosphere which could support life."

"It takes time to heal all wounds," Mylok, the philosopher, stated. "Your people always feared the day of rapture. Yet, they took little action to prevent it."

"It's a good thing that we're here then," Barbara said in relief.

"Barbara, you don't understand," Mylok said alarmed. "Without the Orb of Sun-God Ra, the Tzorb will end and we too will die."

"No," Barbara cried as she listened to him. As she sat back in her chair, Mylok gentle embraced her for support and completed his thoughts. "Again, man's technology surpassed his logic."

Chapter 12

A few more days passed. Barbara's new world encouraged her slowly to forget her old world. Each day she did a little more exploring of Mylok's palace alone. He alone had close to eleven square miles of rooms. She had seen hundreds of rooms. Each one seemed to remind her a bit of her world. Many rooms represented varied cultures and nations from the earth. She never understood how one man could be so intrigued by so many diverse cultures until one day, when she decided to walk into another room.

Barbara looked around the large laboratory. Encased within many enormous crystals were hundreds of men from the past. She walked among the tubes to see many men from different nationalities and civilizations. Each man seemed to be lifeless, but not dead. It seemed as though each was asleep. As she continued to walk, she stopped in front of a tube. Encased within the tube was another body of Mylok.

"Barbara," a voice called her name from behind. The voice startled her. "What are you doing here?" Mylok asked her.

She quickly turned around, believing that one alleged corpse had come to life. She was happy to see that it was the real Mylok. Knowing that she was probably in trouble for snooping around, she hoped to avoid a confrontation by asking him. "Who are these people?"

"Each of them are me," Mylok responded.

"How can they all be you?" she asked.

"Each man has been created by me without a soul," Mylok tried to explain. "I've entered into your world many times through different forms to give knowledge to your people. It was I who gave your people the equation for nuclear power, even though they abused that knowledge."

"You have the power to enter into another man's body?" Barbara asked.

"Yes," he claimed. "My internal energy can be projected into another's body. However, these men have never lived their own life and have no soul. Their cells have been cultivated and built through the changing of my own DNA molecules. It's like building a house to be moved into later."

"Why do you need a back up body of yourself?" she asked.

"In case of an emergency, I can live in the other body while I repair my damaged body," he told her.

"Have you ever had to use your other body?"

"No...I haven't had the need."

"Then what are the other bodies?" Barbara asked. "Vacation homes?"

"Exactly," he said. "Imagine a man entering a culture of prejudice. How could he teach that nation?"

"I guess I understand," she said as she looked at a Chinese man in a tube next to his. "When did you have to use this body?"

"In the teaching of the Shaolin monks to develop their body as a weapon against the overthrow of their Ming Dynasty," Mylok told her.

"The Ming Dynasty was overthrown hundreds of years ago," she said knowingly.

"You can't win them all."

Barbara was shocked by his words. It sounded to her that he claimed to be more than a hundred years old. She had never asked his age before, because she figured him to be no more than in his mid-twenties. Barbara then asked him for the first time, "How old are you?"

"Five thousand three hundred and forty-seven years," Mylok stated.

At first, she was greatly startled. Barbara was speechless. Then, Barbara recalled what Jack Turner had told her at the great dinner party. Jack said that he knew Mylok for over forty years. "I know that the astronauts don't age in space when they traveled to the moon," Barbara said knowingly. "You're telling me that no one ages in your world."

"No," he stated. "I'm the only one. Life from your world would be slightly accelerated here due to this world's being closer to the earth's core. The further down one goes, the greater the gravitational force becomes. Living here would take away about three months of an individual's average life span. At the same time, though, the life span is extended here due to the clean environment."

"How come I haven't noticed the increase in gravity?" she asked.

"That is because it is so slight a change," he told her. "Do you see now why it is impossible for me ever to marry you, Barbara? I barely age a year for every thousand of your years."

"In forty years, I'll be an old woman. What will you think of me then?" she asked.

"I didn't ask you to come here due to your looks," Mylok said. "It is who you are as an individual that attracted me to you. Remember Jack Turner at the great gathering? We have been friends for many years. You have seen how well we treat our elderly people. Their wisdom and experiences are greatly respected. You already know that many of our greatest scientists are over seventy years of age." Mylok continued, "I shall always be with you."

Barbara hesitated in her reply to him, while being greatly touched by his words. Each person within the crystal tubes rested vertically while in suspended animation. After each person had been frozen vertically in hibernation with their backs upon a creation table, the palms of the hands faced outward toward their window enclosures. Even though each of Mylok's creations were clothed, the forearms of the Chinese man were bare, due to the short sleeves of his dress of those ancient times. While pointing at the young Chinese man, Barbara asked, "What are those marks on his arms?"

"Those are brandings," Mylok told her.

"It looks like a dragon and a tiger," she said barely recognizing the marks due to the frost upon the crystal tube. "Why did you brand him?" she asked and then thought again. "If you're he, then you branded yourself. Why? Didn't burning yourself hurt?"

"I showed the Shaolin monks how to control their bodies and minds, therefore eliminating the feeling of all pain," Mylok said. "The final test of a true master of these teachings is to burn the flesh to show that there is control over the feeling of pain."

"So if a monk were to break his leg, he wouldn't be able to feel the pain?" Barbara asked in disbelief.

"At first, he would feel tremendous pain," Mylok tried to explain. "By channeling his thoughts through meditation, one could diminish the sensation." She looked confused, so he continued, "This is much like a person being unable to feel pain while one sleeps. That is why a person is put to sleep before an operation."

"Oh, so when he feels pain, he tries to sleep," she said.

"He meditates," Mylok explained. "The brain is much like any machine. With time, it can be controlled to conform to one's needs and thoughts. For example, if a person was to be stabbed in a fight, he would be able to slow down or even stop the bleeding by slowing down his own heartbeat through the channeling of his thoughts."

"You will have to teach me more about meditating then," she told him. "So, you're also a karate expert."

"Barbara, I was the founder of all martial arts thousands of years ago," Mylok exclaimed.

"Next, you will be telling me that you built the pyramids," she said jokingly. "You sure did well against those street punks on our first date. If you're so good with your hands and feet, why did you get hit?"

"I let him hit me."

"Oh, come on!" she said with disbelief. "Why would anyone be willing to get hit?"

"To disturb his psyche so that he may never again harm another person," Mylok exclaimed. "Imagine the power that hoodlum must have felt after striking me. When he wasn't able to move me, and all of that power was stripped away from him. Surely, you can see that it was more damaging to his mind than never to have that power to begin with."

"I guess I understand," she said. "Didn't it hurt?"

"Not at all," Mylok told her. "That is the power of chi; the inner force." He continued, "By the way, I did not build the pyramids. I designed them."

Barbara giggled over his reply. Then, she looked among Mylok's many "other selves" within the great laboratory. "So, which of these is your original body?" she asked. Barbara believed that it was possible he lived in his current body only so that he could visit America.

"This is my original body," he said while touching his chest with his hands.

"Sorry," she said. "How was I to know? From what you have been telling me, I wasn't sure. You don't look like a typical Egyptian." Barbara always stereotyped an Egyptian as having black hair, brown eyes, and to have dark skin. With Mylok's blue eyes, dark brown hair, and lighter complexion due to the loss of his dark tan through the thousands of years, he looked more like any other nationality.

"I was an Egyptian slave," Mylok told her. "Slaves were taken from all other nations."

"I'm sorry to hear that," Barbara said, knowing the memories must be painful for him. She then recalled the mural of his father and him in the fields of what must have been thousands of slaves. Barbara now believed that his father died as a slave. Barbara did not want to ask, fearing that it would be too painful for him to discuss. Instead, she asked, "Did you ever have any brothers and sisters?"

"Yes, many," he said, remembering them all. "I had three brothers who died by my side in the fields. They died from starvation and thirst. Five of my brothers were slain during the capture of my village. My mother and sisters were never seen or heard from again after the Egyptian invasion."

"You must hate the Egyptians for what they have done to you," Barbara said. "I'm sorry that I have ever mentioned Egypt in the past." Her eyes welled with tears in sympathy to Mylok's pain.

"I don't hate anyone," Mylok said. "On the contrary, I admired their power and am thankful for what they have done for me. If it wasn't for them, I wouldn't have this world or even know you."

As Barbara hugged Mylok to give him what she believed to be needed support, she looked in the massive room at the many people Mylok had once appeared as in her world. "What a waste," she said in his ear. "All your teachings to end in destruction."

Later that day, Barbara went to the Tzorb in search for the Orb of the Sun-God Ra. The Tzorb traveled back in time before her grandfather's death. She watched her cousin Glen appear to play catch with Princess, one of the several dogs on the ranch. However, nothing was thrown. Later, the two appeared to bury something behind the hay barn, though it could not be seen by the Tzorb. "That must be it," Barbara said. "Mylok," she talked to the Tzorb. "I think I found it."

After a few minutes, Mylok appeared in the Tzorb room. He said, "That's it, Barbara. You found the orb."

"What will happen to the world now?"

"Come, I will show you." Mylok then led Barbara through a teleporting doorway.

Barbara looked down a great hallway which reminded her of the tales of Noah's ark she heard as a young girl. It looked like a museum of animals. However, there were millions of different species. There were two of each species: one male and one female, Barbara guessed.

"It hasn't been the first time that life was destroyed on earth," Mylok said. "All the dinosaurs became extinct, as well as the advanced Egyptian race."

"What ever happened to the Egyptians?" Barbara asked him, curious to know the true answer.

"They all died due to a great drought," Mylok answered her.

"Didn't the aliens help them?" she asked.

"No," he said. "Through the years the Egyptians became a very powerful race. The land was fruitful as a result of the aliens' aid. As the Egyptians became knowledgeable from their teachings, they began to believe that they were also becoming gods. Soon the people believed that they no longer needed the aliens, and then they began to fight against them. Our race began to separate into many different nations due to the change in beliefs. My people and I knew they were wrong."

"Then what happened?" she asked.

"A war broke out between the Egyptians and the aliens," he continued. "Due to the people's blasphemy, the aliens left the humans to perish in drought. The once plentiful crops of Egypt were soon to end in dust. Without food and water, the once mighty race quickly died."

"What happened to you and your people?" she asked.

"That's obvious," he stated.

"I guess that wasn't good thinking on my part," she added. "It is obvious that the aliens brought you here. Why here of all places?"

"Because it's the earth's most active location," he reminded her. "Also, so that we could grow in peace."

As they continued walking down another great hallway, she continued to see more unusual animals in groups of two. Each animal was in hibernation. All the creatures would sleep until the day they were needed. Again, Barbara recalled the story of Noah's ark. "These animals. You are going to deposit them on the earth?"

"Yes," Mylok told her. "Even though many of these animals are from different worlds."

"When are you going to set them free?"

"In two weeks," Mylok told her. "Soon, my galactic friends will return to the earth in the aid of the Global Genesis."

"The what?"

"The recreation of this planet, earth."

A week had passed. All the people of Mylok were busy preparing for the Global Genesis. The Orb of Sun-god Ra was retrieved and returned to its origin, as well as the second orb. The four orbs were again in their place around the globe. The Tzorb was hard at work in the taking of the earth's internal energy. The Tzorb soon acted like an air bubble within a glass of water. The buoyancy of the Tzorb within the molten lava soon led the three towers to break through the earth's crust.

Slowly, the twelve mile high towers crept upward through the Atlantic Ocean. Within three days, the three towers stretched seven miles into the dark sky from the ocean's surface. Even though it was high noon, the sky was greatly darkened by black clouds from the asteroid strike.

The darkened atmosphere quickly caused the planet to freeze into an ice world. The Bermuda area alone dropped under thirty degrees Fahrenheit. The few creatures that survived the impact would soon freeze to death. Throughout the world, few buildings remained undamaged.

The entire world had once burned in an uncontrollable fire. Now the atmosphere could no longer sustain any form of life. Even within the oceans, all marine life soon began to perish due to the drastic change in temperature. What took the earth millions of years to balance all life was quickly demolished within a matter of days.

Over the week, Barbara soon realized the true power Mylok possessed. His people knew the secrets to control all the earth's elements.

"I now understand," Barbara said as she saw Mylok turn the element lead into solid gold. "By removing one atomic particle from mercury which has an atomic number of eighty, you create a new number of seventy-nine," she stated, looking at a chart of the elements.

"Correct," Mylok said to her. "Which element has an atomic number of seventy-nine?"

"Gold," she stated while looking at the chart.

"Correct again," Mylok said. "Now if lead has an atomic number of eighty-two, how is it possible to make gold?"

"If gold has an atomic number of seventy-nine, then all I would have to do is to remove three atomic particles," Barbara said. "Is it possible?"

"Yes," he said. "You just saw it with your own eyes."

"Then by changing the number of particles you could create any element that you wish," Barbara said, now knowing the secret to life.

"You now understand," he said. "With these towers it is possible to recreate an atmosphere within a few days that will again sustain life."

"Your people and animals will again roam the earth," she said, hoping to visit the outside world again.

"Yes," Mylok replied. "However, for what we're about to do, the risk is even greater."

"Why?"

"Upon completion of the Global Genesis, my world is going to attempt a dimensional time change to before the destruction of the earth."

"Can you really do this?" Barbara asked. "Can you bring my friends and family back to life."

"There is no death...only different realms of dimensions," Mylok said. "I will tell you one thing. America had lost the last World War. Germany had invented the atomic bomb first and dropped it on New York."

She was in semi-shock to hear that. "So, you have done this before." Barbara knew this to be the truth, because Mylok no longer joked around with the end of his world so near.

The three dark crystal towers soon charged the atmosphere with an infinite number of electrons and protons. Hundreds of thousands of lightning bolts shot from one tower to the other five miles apart, therefore creating new gases that could again support life.

Occasionally, Mylok and Barbara would sit in front of a window to watch the change in atmosphere. Each day the sky became clearer, until one day when they were finally able to see the coast of America. Mylok promised her that someday she would be able to return to America. But to what?

The only world she loved now was Mylok's. Over the years, she would age and soon die. Barbara knew that she could not be with Mylok forever. However, she now knew that she loved Mylok--not Paul.

If the dimensional time travel was to fail, it would take many years to get rid of the rubble and replace it with a new structure. Mylok had already told her that. Worse still, what about her relationship with Mylok? Would that too change, as she grew older over the next few years? How and why would he want to love an old woman?

Chapter 14

A few more days passed. The earth was again greeted by the space travelers from a superior world. Their technology would aid in the rebuilding of a better world. This time without any human sacrifices! There was only the arrival of one small spaceship. The aliens were only to stay a few days to give Mylok some advice and would then depart for their home planet.

Barbara never met the five aliens since the day of their arrival. Their space craft rested upon the top of one of the crystal towers. The aliens' meetings with Mylok were always held in private. Three days had already passed since she had seen Mylok. Barbara spent most of her days alone with Maxalavar, using the Tzorb's computer banks to watch American classic movies from her past on the large TV screen.

Barbara realized that not all her world had vanished. All sights, places, people, and movies of the past were still available through the Tzorb. As the two stuffed their faces with Mylokian food that Maxalavar prepared, they enjoyed some "I Love Lucy" reruns. Barbara tossed the bite sized food into the air to catch it in her mouth. She used to catch peanut M&M's at times with Paul.

Maxalavar's head went up every time Barbara tossed the food into the air. "Strange custom you have," Maxalavar said. Never before had Max seen food eaten in this fashion. Max curled the tip of his prehensile tail to form a type of spoon. While plunging his tail into the bowl of food, he threw the morsel into the air. His head snapped backwards as he watched the food fly over his head. Max then did the same thing two more times. Maxalavar's discouragement led him to increase his odds of catching a piece of food by throwing more into the air.

Barbara laughed hysterically as food was flying everywhere. "Stop it, Max!" she screamed. "You're making a mess."

"Not easy to do," Max said in English. Max then stopped when he saw a figure emerge out of the corner of his eye. Barbara looked upward to see Mylok standing there.

"Leave us," Mylok said to Max in his Mylokian language. Maxalavar quickly left the loving couple alone. Barbara rushed to hug Mylok and then gave him a long, lingering kiss. She had missed not seeing him for three days.

"I missed you so much," Barbara said with joy. She gave him another passionate kiss while hugging him. "I love you so much. I didn't know when you were coming back."

"I love you too, Barbara," Mylok said. He then asked her something that she thought would never cross his lips. "Will you marry me?"

Barbara nearly fainted in his arms upon hearing those words. "I thought it would be impossible," she said.

"I've communicated with my friends," he said with a smile. "They can do for you the same as they have done for me. We will always be together."

"Whether you can bring my world back to me, or not..." Barbara said, willful to give up her friends and family. "Yes, I will marry you."

Mylok brought her willingly to his intimate six fingered friends and left her in their trusted hands. She would soon be like Mylok, having been granted eternal life. However, the trust of the Tzorb's knowledge was left to only one individual: Mylok.

While the aliens performed their operation on Barbara, Mylok awaited the completion of the operation on top of a tower. The roof of the tower alone stretched over three-quarters of a mile.

While inside a dome covered room, Mylok watched. The earth's atmosphere was cleaner than ever before. The top of the towers stretched seven miles high from the Atlantic's surface. The sky around burned with an unearthly fire between the three towers. This fire became the most breathtaking rainbow in the world. An enormous halo formed around the three crystalline towers. Then, the completion of the dimensional time travel was finally accomplished. It was successful!

The sky became black. Suddenly, the stars became visible to the naked eye. A full moon shone within the midnight sky. Again from ages past, the face of Mylok's father shone from the moon's surface.

Mylok raised his hands toward the moon, remembering what his father had once told him. "Father, I shall soon have a family," he said in his native Mylokian tongue. "Now, it is time to rebuild this world the right way!" In a soft voice he added, "The next evolution of humankind shall soon begin..."

The End

Although I may be unable to write back to everyone, I would enjoy to hear from you. If you have any questions or comments, you can write me at the following address:

Thorpe Wright
PO Box 197
Auburndale, MA 02466
USA

Email: thor_337@hotmail.com

About the Author

Thorpe ("Thor") E. Wright V, is a descendant of British royalty from the House of Thorpe. Thor spent his early teenage summers as a cattle rancher. Being raised in the suburbs of Boston, Massachusetts, USA, he is a graduate of Assumption College with a B. A. in Business Management and a minor in Computer Science. For fourteen years, Mr. Wright worked as a motion picture operations manager/projectionist for the largest theatre chain in the Boston area. Thor obtained a CDL A license, and later drove a 53' tractor/trailer across the USA for two years.

As an eclectic martial artist with over forty-three years experience, Thor taught Kempo karate for ten years, and later co-founded the Cambridge Institute of Martial Arts (CIMA). He is proficient in many forms of eastern meditation, and is an astral traveler. As president of ThaiCat Productions, Shihan Wright hopes to someday syndicate his own TV show to educate people about the variety of martial arts and teach eastern philosophies.

Thorpe Wright is posted on the Internet Movie Data base @ www. IMDb.com as an executive producer, and a technical advisor, for two independent films.

Thor has spent a year in writing his third book. Currently self-employed and a bachelor, Mr. Wright lives near Boston, MA--not far from the Boston Museum of Science and the beautiful Charles River.

Printed in the United States
By Bookmasters